MEET THE FOUNDING MEMBERS
OF THE ZODIAC CLUB

ABBY MARTIN: A typical *Aries,* Abby brings the Zodiac Club together. She's always prepared to help others, but her headstrong Aries nature sometimes gets in her way. Will her wild and wonderful whims prevail?

MARA BENNETT: Feminine and charming, she personifies the *Libra* spirit. She appreciates harmony, but it is difficult for her to make a decision. How can she become more decisive?

J. L. RICHTER: Makes cool *Scorpio* a reality with her aloof and independent spirit. Like all Scorpios, she's sure of what she wants and determined to get it. But what is the cost?

ELIZABETH LEONARD: A true *Pisces,* she's a friend who's easily trusted, but her trust in others leaves her vulnerable to being hurt. She has dreams of her own and for every friend in the club. But who comes first?

CATHY ROSEN: Makes her *Leo* sign ring true with confidence and charisma, but her eagerness for praise often overshadows her accomplishments!

JESSICA HOLLY: The friendly, outgoing *Virgo* dreams of finding the right boy and wonders if she'll find a Prince Charming who will meet her expectations. Will her yearnings ever be fulfilled?

PENNY ROSS: A whiz at tennis, she's the perfect *Sagittarius*—zany but endearing! With her flair on the court and her fierce loyalty to her friends, she's just not made for the ordinary, but will she make a superstar?

J.L. Richter

Mara Bennett

Elizabeth Leonard

Abby Martin

Jessica Holly

Cathy Rosen

Penny Ross

AQUARIUS AHOY!

Including zodiac vacation spots

S. J. Lawrence

 **BOOKS FOR YOUNG ADULTS**

a member of The Putnam Publishing Group
NEW YORK

Published by Pacer Books,
a member of The Putnam Publishing Group
51 Madison Avenue
New York, New York 10010

ISBN: 0-399-21222-1

RL: 5.8
Pacer is a trademark of The Putnam Publishing Group.
The Zodiac Club is a trademark of The Putnam
Publishing Group.

Printed in the United States of America
First printing

AQUARIUS AHOY!

AQUARIUS (*January 20–February 18*)

RULING PLANET: *Uranus*   SYMBOL: *The Water Bearer*

★ ────────────────

As an Aquarius girl you are forever chasing rainbows and need a mate who can deal with sudden changes. Your perfect mate must be as curious and ready to adapt as you are. Watch out for tendencies to hide your emotions. It's not that you're uncaring, you're just restless. Don't give your love to someone just to prove a point to someone else. You're intuitive and a charmer, but often seem in another world. Look for love among your friends or other groups with high ideals. Love can surprise you, happily.

★ ────────────────

RELATIONSHIPS:

Aquarius & Aries—a surprising combination, good or bad

Aquarius & Taurus—better for friendship, not passion

Aquarius & Gemini—a meeting of minds, often very good

Aquarius & Cancer—good for friendship, not romance

Aquarius & Leo—each needs the other

Aquarius & Virgo—solid relationship, but little passion

Aquarius & Libra—never a dull moment, the best bet

Aquarius & Scorpio—a need for respect here for lasting love

Aquarius & Sagittarius—love is an adventure

Aquarius & Capricorn—definite attraction, with differences

Aquarius & Aquarius—similar objectives, can be excellent

Aquarius & Pisces—friendship here, but rarely romance

1

"Three hours ago in New York, it was twenty-five degrees and snowing like crazy," J.L. Richter exclaimed.

"We have begun our final approach into Miami International Airport," the cheery voice of the stewardess announced. "The temperature is seventy-two degrees and the skies are fair."

J.L. and her friends Jessica Holly and Penny Ross leaned eagerly toward the plane window. "Mr. Richter, I think I see my first palm tree!" Jessica called to J.L.'s father, who was seated with J.L.'s mother in the row behind. "This is so great! I can't believe we're really in Florida."

J.L. nudged Penny and smiled. "She hasn't been able to tear herself away from the window this whole trip," she whispered, just loud enough for Jessica to hear.

Penny laughed. "She must have spotted a good-looking guy in a passing plane! Take a look, J.L. Let me know if he's worth checking out."

"Hey, you guys . . . ," Jessica began, wheeling around indignantly. J.L. tried hard to keep from laughing when she saw Jessica's friendly green eyes flash in protest.

"It's all right, Jess. Believe me, we're as excited as you are," J.L. said reassuringly.

Jessica blushed. "Well, I guess I am a little too enthusiastic," she admitted. "But you should look out there. It's lush and green—not a drop of snow!" She turned back to the window, unable to contain herself.

"I wouldn't mind looking, Jess," J.L. said, "but it's not so easy—your red hair is totally blocking the window."

"Sorry." Jessica sat back far enough to allow her friends a view. J.L. leaned across to see the coastline below. As the plane descended, J.L. actually thought she could make out people sunbathing on the beach. She stretched her arms and tossed her thick, dark hair.

"I can't wait to get out in the Florida sunshine," she purred in her husky voice. "I'm as white as the Collingwood snow," she added, rolling up a sleeve and looking at her forearm.

"We'll be in Miami soon," J.L. continued, "but then we have the drive to the Keys. My father says it will take another three hours, maybe a little more." She paused and glanced at her watch. "Hmm. Ten twenty. We might be able to catch some rays in Duck Key this afternoon."

"Look at the size of that yacht," Penny whistled.

"What do you mean, yacht? That's an ocean liner!" Jessica countered.

J.L. chuckled to herself. She turned around and glanced at her parents. She was met by her father's warm smile.

"Well, Jocelyn, how do you feel now?" Mr. Richter teased his obviously thrilled daughter.

"I can't complain," J.L. stammered, looking from her father to her mother. "This all happened so fast! Everything seemed too good to be true. It's a miracle that I even managed to pack. But," she added, beaming at her father, "Tuesday, February 16, is one day I'll never forget."

J.L. had been staring at her math book, unable to concentrate. She clapped her hands over her eyes in frustration. This stuff makes absolutely no sense to me, she thought to herself.

In her best imitation robot voice, she said, *"I cannot complete the task you have assigned me. Does not compute. Does not compute."* She laughed for a second, then crossed to her bedroom window.

"I think Mr. Anderson is determined to ruin my junior year of high school," J.L. muttered. She stared out the window and thought about her day. Her horoscope from the morning paper had been intriguing: *"February 16: Scorpio* (Oct. 23–Nov. 22): *Hard work on an old problem finally pays off. Family member has a surprise in store."*

No doubt about it, math was the "old problem." "But," she grumbled, "I don't think hard work will help this time. This geometry and math in general will take a miracle to solve."

Outside, everything was buried in a thick covering of snow. It was only four thirty in the afternoon, and already the streetlights were on in Collingwood. Winter, she thought. How depressing!

As she sat back down at her desk, J.L. heard her father's forceful voice calling from downstairs.

"Jocelyn? Jocelyn, come here, will you?"

"Coming, Dad," she answered, glancing at her clock. "Four thirty-five. What's Dad doing home so early?" Her father usually put in long days at his New York City office. All those hours had paid off—David Richter was a senior partner in a stockbrokerage firm and one of Collingwood's most prominent residents. For J.L., her father's business success had one big drawback— she hardly ever saw him.

Still preoccupied with her miserable homework situation, J.L. came down the stairs heavily. "Hi, Dad," she managed to say with a smile. "How was your day?"

"Fine, Jocelyn, just fine, but what's the matter with you? It looks like you're carrying the weight of the world."

J.L. smiled at her father. It didn't seem to matter how little they saw of each other; he could always see her moods through her cool Scorpio exterior.

"Oh, nothing, Dad. I mean, just the same old story. Mr. Anderson gave another impossible geometry assignment and it's driving me crazy."

"Sounds to me like you could use some cheering up."

"I sure could," J.L. muttered, looking toward the front window. Don't get all worked up over nothing, she warned herself, hoping her father had brought home a surprise for her. Those little things in the paper are hardly ever accurate. And Dad isn't exactly a man of many surprises.

When J.L. looked up into her father's eyes, she noticed a lighthearted twinkle that was rarely there. Whatever he had on his mind this evening, J.L. was sure it wasn't business. She could feel excitement knotting up in her stomach.

"What is it, Dad?" J.L. asked.

"Well, Jocelyn, I meant to wait and tell you at dinner," her father answered, adding shyly, "but I guess I just can't keep a secret anymore."

J.L. pleaded. "Keep what secret? Dad, please tell me what it is."

"You know Bob Taylor from my office? He has a fishing cottage in the Florida Keys and was planning to take his family there for the long Presidents' Day weekend—that's this weekend—but it seems he can't make it after all . . ."

"Yes?" J.L. interrupted excitedly.

". . . and since he already had the low-fare airline reservations, he offered them to us. What do you think, Jocelyn? I'd like to take you and your mother there for the weekend and get away from all this cursed snow."

J.L. started to answer, but her mouth couldn't seem to think of any words.

"That is, if you don't mind."

"Mind? *Mind?* It's wonderful!" J.L. shouted as she threw her arms around her father.

"Well, isn't this a lovely picture," said Anne Richter as she appeared at the door. She looked from her tall and handsome husband to her daughter, who had inherited his good looks. "Jocelyn, dear, what *are* you so *happy* about?" she teased, exaggerating her natural, but fading, Southern accent.

"Didn't Dad tell you, Mother?"

Anne Richter laughed. "He told me today over the phone. *I* wasn't supposed to tell you. But it seems your father is the one who couldn't wait. . . . Do you think Penny and Jessica will be able to come?"

J.L. jumped. "What?"

Her father broke in, turning toward his wife. "I hadn't reached that part yet, Anne."

"So much for keeping secrets," Mrs. Richter laughed.

"Jocelyn, Bob Taylor made plane reservations for five. I said yes to all five tickets, so you can invite two friends. He smiled, adding, "If that's all right, too?"

J.L. was just beginning to get over the shock. "Well, I . . . I . . . Yes, I suppose that would . . . would be . . ." she stammered, then broke out laughing. "Oh, Dad, thank you! Penny and Jessica were going to sleep over this weekend and I'm sure they won't mind switching from Collingwood to the Florida Keys!"

When she climbed the stairs to her room, J.L. felt as if she were floating. Her desk lamp still shone on her open geometry book. The triangles on the page now suggested tall, billowed sails floating on the sea.

"Only four days!" J.L. realized when she looked up at the calendar over her desk. "I'd better call Jessica and Penny!"

J.L.'s eyes fell on the photograph over her bed. It was her favorite picture. She laughed everytime she looked at the photo of the Zodiac Club. There they were, her best friends in the world, pretending to be different figures from the zodiac. "I wish I could invite all of them," J.L. said aloud as she plopped down on her bed.

Being part of this group was new for J.L. and she was loving it. In the beginning, making friends at Collingwood High was hard. There was the rivalry that existed in Collingwood between the kids from the "River" area of town and kids from the "Hill." To make matters worse, J.L.'s family lived in the nicest neighborhood on the Hill. Many kids automatically assumed that she and her close friends Penny Ross and Mara Bennett were just typical "Hill snobs."

Life changed after her summer at Spruce Hill Camp. J.L. had worked with Abby Martin last summer and they became friends. Abby introduced her to her friends Cathy Rosen, Jessica Holly, and Elizabeth Leonard. J.L. was grateful that there were people who could see that there was something to her besides money. However, at times like this, J.L. still feared that her family's money and the special things that it bought might come between her and her friends.

J.L. was worried. "Since I've already asked Penny and Jessica to sleep over this weekend, it's logical that I should invite them, isn't it?" She was afraid that someone would be mad at her for not being asked.

"What am I doing?" she chided herself. "Here I am worrying, when I just got the greatest news anyone could ask for!"

J.L. went to the phone and quickly dialed Penny's number.

"Penny, it's J.L."

"Oh, hi, J.L. What's up?"

"You're not going to believe this, Penny," J.L. began, barely able to keep her voice from rising over its normal, slightly husky pitch. "You remember I invited you to sleep over Saturday night?"

"Sure I do. Why, is something wrong?"

"Hardly," J.L. laughed and went on, "I was just wondering if you'd like to stay with us Friday and Sunday nights too—in the Florida Keys!"

"What?" Penny shouted in disbelief. "J.L., is this some kind of joke?"

"Penny Ross, J.L. Richter does not make jokes!"

"Well, what are you talking about?" Penny finally managed to ask.

"Here's the story." J.L. explained exactly what her father had told her.

Penny, who had barely been able to contain herself, burst out, "You're kidding. J.L., you're kidding!"

"J.L. Richter does not kid!"

"A whole weekend?" Penny asked. "Oh, J.L., I want to go so bad, and I know I could probably convince my parents, but I'm going to have to call my coach. I have a feeling he's not going to be thrilled about a four-day stretch without a tennis lesson."

J.L. frowned. She knew Penny would give up many things to keep in training. But she couldn't help sounding disappointed. "C'mon, Penny. You need the break. Tell your coach it's a once-in-a-lifetime chance. Tell him you deserve some time with your friends. I'll practice with you. My game isn't great, but you can keep up your work. Please, Penny?"

Penny laughed. "You can bet I'll do my best," she promised.

"Call me back, okay?"

J.L. immediately dialed Jessica's number. A cheerful voice answered the phone.

"Jessica, it's J.L.," she began.

"No," Mrs. Holly laughed. Since Jessica was in eighth grade, she had been confused with her daughter on the phone. "I'll call Jessica."

"Sorry, Mrs. Holly."

Jessica picked up the extension. "J.L.?"

"Jessica, is that really you?" J.L. asked cautiously.

"Of course, you fool. What's up?"

"I've got a proposition."

"No, J.L., I will not do the next take-home geometry test in exchange for three inches of your height," Jessica said.

"Nice guess, Jessica, but wrong. How would you like to trade your overnight at the Richter home for an all-expense-paid, four-day, three-night trip to the Florida Keys?"

"Hmm. Well, yes, well, no, well, ah *sold!*" laughed Jessica, not believing her friend's offer.

"Great!" J.L. said. "Okay. I think Dad said the flight leaves from New York at eight thirty in the morning, so we'll have to pick you up really early—I'll tell you an exact time tomorrow at school. Pack summer clothes, but only a weekend's worth. We'll come back Monday afternoon. . . . If there's anything I forgot—"

"Whoa, wait a minute, J.L.," Jessica broke in. "I think it sounds like you're serious."

"Of course I'm serious, Jessica."

"You're not kidding?"

J.L. sighed heavily. "Now you sound just like Penny!"

"Really, J.L., what's the story?"

J.L. quickly related the details of her father's offer. When she finished, there was silence at the other end of the phone. "Jessica, are you there?" J.L. asked.

"I'm so excited I'm speechless!" Jessica finally replied. "Now that I realize you're serious, J.L., I'll ask my parents. Hang on, okay?"

J.L. waited for what seemed an eternity. When

Jessica's voice came through the phone again, J.L. immediately knew the answer was yes.

"All right!" J.L. exclaimed. She hung up the phone, but it rang almost immediately.

"Penny?" she asked.

"Hi, J.L."

"Well, Penny?"

"Well, yes!"

"Yes?"

"Yes! J.L., I'm so psyched for this. Can Jessica go?"

"Yep," J.L. answered. "Penny, this is going to be so great! My horoscope was right for once."

"Wait until the other Zodiacs find out. They'll be crazy with envy," Penny said, laughing.

"They'll be happy for us too," J.L. answered.

"Oh, I know that," Penny replied. "But they'll die when they see our winter tans!"

Everything was settled. J.L. hung up the receiver and went to her bookshelf. As soon as she found her tattered atlas, she opened it to the Florida spread. With her finger, J.L. followed the outline of the state all the way to its southern tip. Starting there, a thin line of islands curved back into the Gulf of Mexico, like a claw on a cat's paw. It was going to be great. "Florida Keys, here we come!" she announced.

2

The plane touched down on the runway and coasted to the gate. The flight was crowded, and for several minutes the aisles were jammed with passengers gathering their carry-on bags.

"I can't believe we were lucky enough to find this article on perfect vacation spots for each sign in this airline magazine," Jessica said.

"I don't think anyone will mind if we take the article," Penny added. "After all, it's a free magazine that they use for advertising."

"The list is great," J.L. said as she took one last glance before they were able to get into the aisle.

Star-Studded Vacation Spots

ARIES—*The Ram: March 21–April 20*
A jaunt through Mexico or a bike trip across America

is the perfect vacation for the Ram. The Aries nature loves impulsiveness and change. Stop at Yellowstone National Park to see Old Faithful and don't miss the Mount Saint Helens area. Volcanoes intrigue the fiery Aries.

TAURUS—*The Bull: April 21–May 20*
New Orleans, with its Cajun French culture, is the ideal place for the romantic side of Taurus. Visit the countryside of England with its beautiful gardens and opportunities for hiking. Although the Bull is a home-body and would prefer to stay in familiar surroundings, the similarity of the language and the land makes Great Britain a perfect Taurus trip.

GEMINI—*The Twins: May 21–June 20*
The perfect place for a Gemini to go is *anywhere*. The Gemini gift for languages and natural ability to make friends suggests foreign travel. Try a course at the Sorbonne in France, live with a family in Egypt, or join an African safari. Activity and adventure are sure to please this sign.

CANCER—*The Crab: June 21–July 20*
America's sign is Cancer, and so the most natural vacation places for the Crab are in the United States. San Francisco is the city to visit during the summer, or Washington, D.C. In the winter, Florida with its sea-side resorts, miles of beaches, is the right place for this sign to bask in the sun.

LEO—*The Lion: July 21–August 21*

The perfect vacation for the Lion is, of course, a trip to Africa—a chance to explore the world of Kenya or Ghana. The cost of a real safari might be out of the question, but inventive Leos might enjoy a long camping trip in the Southwest or a rafting trip down the Colorado river.

VIRGO—*The Virgin: August 22–September 22*

A summer trip to Alaska or Scandinavia is ideal for Virgos, who get a kick out of seeing the wonders of nature. The midnight sun, an awe-inspiring mountain range, or a volcano gives the Virgo enormous pleasure. Visit the ruins of Pompeii or Hawaii's Volcanoes National Park.

LIBRA—*The Scales: September 23–October 22*

Libras love parties and people, and their vacations should be full of both. Travel with a companion who is not a Libra for help with all those impossible decisions— where to go, what to do, how to get there. Paris is a great city for a Libra vacation—beautiful buildings, fashionable people, museums, and shopping! Libras love luxury, so cities and towns are better than lonely country retreats.

SCORPIO—*The Scorpion: October 23–November 22*

Sojourn on a Caribbean island with palm trees, lush vegetables, and hot and humid weather. Fishing and scuba diving have great appeal. For a real Scorpio fantasy, try leading a trip down the Amazon.

SAGITTARIUS—*The Archer:*
November 23–December 20

The born traveler of the zodiac, Sagittarius loves exotic and adventurous places. Cheerfulness and good nature make you as much at home in crowded urban settings as in nature's wild outdoors. Visit the bazaars of the Middle East, Hong Kong, or Tokyo, or plan a trip to the Rocky Mountains.

CAPRICORN—*The Goat: December 21–January 19*

Capricorns do not love to travel, so an ideal vacation spot is a beloved place like an old family cottage in the hills of New Hampshire. If you do get the travel bug, you will surely pick mountainous terrain. Choose the rocky shores of Maine or the English Lake District, where you can view the scenery that inspired poets.

AQUARIUS—*The Water Bearer:*
January 20–February 18

The Water Bearer thrives on contact with new people and new cultures. The Aquarian is more interested in seeing how people live than just playing tourist and taking in the attractions. In the United States, join the hang gliders off the cliffs of San Diego. Any vacation that involves an unusual mode of transportation is for you—a trip on the Concorde to London, a ballooning expedition, or a sail around the Greek isles.

PISCES—*The Fish: February 19–March 20*

Like other water signs, you love to be near the ocean.

For a perfect holiday, go to the French Riviera or spend a summer vacation on Cape Cod. People are important to you, in spite of your need for solitude, so wherever you go, there should be a good social life. Dancing is a favorite Pisces pastime, so look for evening entertainment.

J.L. slipped the magazine with the article into her bag. "At least I'll have something special to give to the other Zodiacs since they all couldn't come on this trip."

When there was finally enough room to move around, Jessica, J.L., and Penny grabbed their bags and hurried toward the door of the plane. Mrs. Richter went to pick up the rental car while Mr. Richter rounded up the herd of bags the group had brought. Just as the clerk handed Mrs. Richter the set of keys, Mr. Richter approached. He was trailed by a harried skycap with a cart full of baggage. David Richter did not look happy.

"We're short one bag, Anne," he explained, glancing toward the girls. "I think it's Jessica's suitcase. I told them I'd have their heads if they don't find it, but it turns out it's still in New York. They told me they would send it down on the next flight—it will get here this evening. Why do vacations always begin this way?"

"They won't bring it down until tonight?"

"No, I'm afraid not. Anyway, there's no point in

waiting around. Is the car all set? All right, J.L., Penny, Jessica, everyone grabs her own bag . . . er, except you, Jessica."

"Oh, great, just my luck," Jessica groaned. "What will I wear?"

The group of five, minus Jessica's bag, stepped out into the bright Florida sunshine. They loaded the trunk and Mr. Richter guided the car onto the freeway, heading south toward the Keys. He turned on the radio, tuned in the noontime news, and soon became lost in the stock-market report. In the back seat, the girls started to object, but soon became involved in their own conversation.

After an hour's drive, Mr. Richter explained, "Anne, girls, this is where we catch the Overseas Highway. This is the first of the Keys, Key Largo." They turned onto the famous road, which cut the long strip of land right down the middle. As they drove, heavily developed resort towns alternated with woods. At first Jessica was only able to catch brief glimpses of the ocean beyond the towns on her side of the car, and Penny occasionally spotted the Gulf of Mexico through the other window. But gradually Key Largo's strip of land narrowed, towns became rarer, and the two great bodies of water came closer and closer together. Suddenly they met ahead, in the distance.

"Whoa, look at that!" J.L. exclaimed, leaning over the front seat and staring out the windshield. As the car moved out onto the first of the miraculous line of bridges that span the tiny islands of the Florida Keys, the girls saw far in the distance a few low, bluish humps, the nearest Keys to the mainland. After passing one island, they soon found themselves on another bridge, twice as long as the first one.

"Look, you guys," Jessica exclaimed, "the water is all different colors. It must be the way the light is hitting it. It's pink over there, and green as an emerald off to the right."

Mr. Richter laughed; then his voice took on the tone of a teacher. "Jessica, that's not the light. What you're seeing is coral. This highway connecting the Keys follows along the only coral reef in the continental United States."

"Yeah, we're on a two-lane bridge a hundred feet above the water," J.L. added, feeling a little sick. "How old is this thing, anyway?"

"This used to be a railroad bridge, built back around the turn of the century. When cars became the prevalent mode of transportation, they simply converted this bridge by laying a highway across the top of it."

"Which makes it over eighty years old, J.L.," Jessica observed playfully.

"Thanks, Jessica. But that's a math problem I can solve myself," J.L. retorted. Then her face began to look serious again, her dark features pulled into a tense expression. "Eighty years old, though—are you sure it's safe, Dad?"

Mr. Richter laughed. "Jocelyn, they've replaced most

of the original bridge by now. I wouldn't worry about it."

As he spoke, they passed onto another of the Keys, a tiny island about the size of a city block. A few houses stood in clearings in the thick palm and mangrove forest. The girls watched huge, strange birds soaring out over the water. Then they passed onto another bridge.

Mrs. Richter suddenly announced, "The next one should be Duck Key." She pointed at a distant island and then at the map on her lap. "This is it."

They turned off the highway onto a smaller bridge, and soon entered a small village on the ocean side of the island. Mr. Richter smiled as he recognized a café and gas station on the right.

"Here we are. I think I'll pull in here and fill up," he called to the back seat. "Why don't you three jump out and take a walk to the house. It's not far—just at the end of Barracuda Road. The car will be in the driveway by the time you get there. Jocelyn, if you want, I'll draw a quick map for you."

J.L. leaned against the car, waiting as her father scrawled a sketchy map on the back of a paper bag. Jessica and Penny started on ahead, and J.L. watched them laughing and jostling each other, Penny's tall figure striding athletically beside Jessica. At one point Penny leaned down and whispered something to Jessica, which seemed to launch both girls into fits of laughter. J.L. smiled to herself. Penny Ross and Jessica

Holly, she thought. Between the two of them there ought to be enough laughs this weekend to last all year. . . .

"Here we are, Jocelyn," Mr. Richter called. J.L. turned toward him, still smiling over her thoughts. "Well, you certainly look happier than I've seen you looking in weeks!"

J.L. crossed to her father and grabbed him around the shoulders. "Oh, Dad, it's just so great that you let me invite both Penny and Jessica. I know how much they appreciate it, too."

Mr. Richter shaded his eyes and looked for the girls. "Well, they're headed in the wrong direction, but that's all right. Jocelyn, here's a rough map. Not that you'll need it. Not much land to get lost on out here. See you in a few minutes."

"Sure, Dad. And thanks for letting us off so we can walk. Seems like I've been sitting forever," J.L. called over her shoulder as she started off after Jessica and Penny. With her long legs and cool but determined stride, she caught up with the other two at an intersection marked by tall palm trees. A warm, steady sea breeze, heavy with the smell of salt, blew across J.L.'s face.

As J.L. approached, Penny and Jessica suddenly broke off their conversation and glanced at each other nervously.

"Am I interrupting anything?" J.L. asked. She had the feeling she was the topic of conversation.

"Oh, nothing, J.L.," Jessica mumbled.

"No, really, J.L., we were just going over the stock-market reports. You know, I'm just amazed that GM went up one and a quarter points today," Penny announced.

"Oh-oh," Jessica jumped in nervously, trying to change the subject. "Can you believe these palm trees? It reminds me of Fantasy Island or something."

J.L. chuckled, still looking at Penny. "Oh, Jess, don't worry about it. It's all part of Penny's perfectly Sagittarian way of not quite realizing what she's saying. Luckily it's not in my Scorpio nature to be offended easily."

Penny returned J.L.'s warm smile. "No, J.L., we were just saying that it's nice to get out and walk for a while. Between the flight and the drive, it feels like we've been sitting for hours—"

"—and she's restless as a Sagittarius, too," Jessica teased.

The three girls laughed and relaxed again. The sun shone brilliantly, and as they walked, they began to pay more attention to Duck Key itself. The town was mostly a collection of two-story frame houses and a few other old, weathered buildings clumped on the ocean side of the Key. Soon they were heading into the breeze, straight toward the ocean. J.L. tilted her head back so the rush of air swept across her face. She looked back at her friends and sighed.

"You know, I really wish all the Zodiacs could be

here. This is so beautiful, but I keep thinking about Abby, Elizabeth, Cathy, and all the others trudging around in all that snow."

"I know what you mean, J.L.," Penny agreed. Can you imagine if we were all together? We'd sure give the Florida Keys a weekend to remember!"

"J.L., you shouldn't feel bad about not being able to invite everyone," Jessica said when she saw the look of concern on J.L.'s face. "Besides, this is a busy weekend for everyone. Mara's skiing with her family, Cathy went to visit her grandparents—almost everyone had plans. In fact, you're just lucky Penny and I could squeeze a trip in this weekend, or you'd be forced to endure *all this* by yourself."

J.L. laughed and broke into a run. As they reached the corner, the girls gasped at the breathtaking sight. A beautiful beach sloped away from them toward the water, practically empty in spite of the perfect weather. Behind them, a few small houses seemed to crouch in among the palms and mangroves. To their right, they could see the Duck Key Marina, where a seemingly endless variety of fishing boats were docked. And right in front of them, the clear blue water gently rubbed against the sand.

Jessica nearly screamed with delight. "This is totally beautiful! I can't believe it! I feel like throwing off my clothes, running down, and diving in right now," she cried, pretending to open the top buttons on her blouse.

Penny turned to J.L. and muttered loud enough for

Jessica to hear, "Typical Jessica Holly move. She can't wait to show off her beautiful body."

"You're right, Penny," Jessica roared. "I definitely feel Venus rising today and romance on the way. C'mon, let's do it!"

J.L. laughed so hard tears rolled down her cheeks. "Jessica, has there ever been a day when you haven't felt Venus rising?"

"Once, I think, in 1978," Jessica retorted.

"J.L., I think Jessica's right about the swimming idea, though," Penny said enthusiastically. "Why don't we head to the house, put on our suits, and hit the beach!"

"But, Jessica, what about your bag?" J.L. asked, more seriously.

"Oh, no!" Jessica groaned, sinking onto a rock overlooking the beach. "My bathing suit! All my clothes! And my astrology guide!"

Penny laughed. "Some Virgo you are. We were counting on that Virgo reliability when we decided that you'd bring the book. If you were really organized, you would have carried your suit and the book in your carry-on bag. Anyway, you can borrow one of my suits."

Jessica smiled sheepishly. "Sorry, guys. But you know me better than that. I didn't pack until late last night, and I just threw everything together. I'm not even sure what I packed—a bikini or a down jacket!"

J.L. and Penny sat down next to Jessica on the rock.

The nearly empty beach stretched out before them, and the calm sea gently lapped against it. J.L. kicked off her shoes and stretched her tall frame over the rock, rolling her shirt up over her belly and her pants up to her knees. Penny followed, but Jessica remained perched at the top of the rock, facing the sea. Several minutes passed, and nobody spoke.

"It's so warm," J.L. finally said.

"Yeah," Penny purred, "and there are hours of sunlight left to soak up this afternoon."

"Can you believe it's February?" Jessica asked.

J.L. shaded her eyes and looked into the sky. "February 18. The sun's still in Aquarius. You know what that means. . . ."

"Yeah, meeting new people, travel, all kinds of new adventures! You guys, this is so exciting," Jessica cried, and suddenly jumped up. Without a word, she crossed the street and disappeared into a small grocery store.

"Beats me." J.L. shrugged, answering Penny's questioning look. Before long, though, Jessica was back, smiling and carrying a local newspaper. She already had it open to the page that had their horoscopes for the day, and she plopped down triumphantly.

Noting the curious expressions on the faces of her companions, she explained, "Well, the book may be in my bag, but this is the next best thing! Who wants to hear their horoscope first?"

"Read J.L.'s," Penny urged Jessica. "After all, she's responsible for us being here, so our fortunes depend on hers this weekend."

"You're right about that, Penny. Now, J.L.," Jessica continued, turning her green eyes to the tall brunette, who propped herself up on an elbow. "Here's your horoscope. *'Scorpio: You may promise and commit yourself to an uncomfortable situation. Evening is ideal for romance, courtship, creative activities, seeing people in groups. Possible conflict with authority figures.'*"

"Hmm," J.L. mused, dropping back to catch the sun. "Ideal for romance, eh?"

Penny laughed, then turned to Jessica excitedly. "Read yours," Penny urged.

"All right, here goes. *'Virgo: You gain from taking a peaceful, amicable, and cooperative attitude. You will meet someone, but may get more from a quiet atmosphere where you can really talk to those you love. Moon in opposition to Mars indicates stressful situations might lead to physical complications.'*" She looked up at her friends and sighed melodramatically. "Oh, yes, the old 'you-will-meet-a-tall-dark-stranger' line."

J.L. propped herself up again. "How about Penny's, Jess?"

"*'Sagittarius: There may be opposition to your plans this weekend. A party held this evening might be more rewarding than one held over the next four evenings. Confusion in romantic scene may cause entanglements with a true friend.'*"

"Oh-oh, you guys," Penny laughed, glancing at her two friends.

J.L. sat up, her excitement obvious in her dark eyes. She smiled in a devilish way. "I think this is going to be a weekend to remember," she announced.

"Maybe so, J.L." Jessica said. But don't you think we should be catching up with your parents at the house?" she added nervously.

"Can't I just have a few more minutes in this sun?" J.L. begged.

"Oh, J.L.," Jessica chided her friend, "you're already tanner from these few minutes in the sun than I'll get all weekend. I just roast and peel, roast and peel."

"What's up for this afternoon?" Penny laughed as the girls got to their feet and started back up the road in the direction Mr. Richter had indicated.

"I think Dad mentioned something about 'a little fishing expedition' for all of us," J.L. moaned.

"That'd be fun!" exclaimed Penny.

Jessica looked at J.L. "You don't sound so excited about it, though," she observed.

J.L. wrinkled her nose. "Well, first of all, I object to the whole idea of fishing. And second of all," she added, her voice taking on a confidential note, "my father's 'fishing expeditions' have a way of turning into disasters."

Jessica laughed and said, "Well, I love a disaster. Let's go!"

3

J.L., Jessica, and Penny walked along the criss-crossing docks of the marina, surrounded by the fleet of commercial fishing boats. Everywhere they looked, the painted hulls gleamed in the sun. Three deeply tanned men passed them, struggling with a basket overflowing with mackerel. The smell of fish was so powerful J.L. wrinkled her nose involuntarily.

As the three girls moved down the docks, followed by J.L.'s parents, fishermen stared at the group of strangers as if they were trying to place them. Jessica felt especially self-conscious in her borrowed clothes. J.L.'s khaki shorts were way too big, and Penny's white shirt could almost have been a minidress. She sensed the curious stares of the fishermen and instinctively slunk into the middle of the group.

"Which one of these old tubs are we going out on?" she whispered nervously, turning from one worn boat to another.

"There she is, over there," Mr. Richter announced, pointing in the direction of a sparkling new boat tied at the end of the dock.

Jessica let out a sigh of relief. Moored between two larger deep-sea-fishing vessels, the open boat Mr. Richter had pointed out looked small, but very new and seaworthy. Its silver outboard motor was tilted up from the water.

"What kind of boat is it?" Penny asked curiously.

Mr. Richter moved closer to the girls, obviously pleased to have another opportunity to educate them. "This is a skiff, a small boat with a flat deck and flat bottom, designed to navigate in shallow waters like these."

"The *Dow Jones*," Jessica giggled, reading the name painted on the stern.

Mr. Richter laughed. "Good old Bob. I don't think he ever stops thinking about the stock market!"

J.L. smiled secretively at her two friends. It was amusing to hear her father speak of his friend Bob Taylor as being overly enthusiastic about his job. As if you're not the same way, she thought.

"This looks a little safer than some of those others, anyway," Jessica declared, bounding aboard. "I guess I expected the boats here would be huge, shining mahogany yachts with perfectly dressed people lounging on the decks, sipping cocktails."

J.L. followed her aboard. "You watch too much TV, Jess," she chided.

"You're right, though, Jessica," Penny added. "I feel so out of place here. These men all look so serious, and I think we're the only girls in the marina."

J.L. surveyed the other boats from the deck of the *Dow Jones* and shrugged in frustration. "Yeah, the only girls in the middle of a hundred men, and all of them over forty. I think this is going to be a waste of time," she muttered under her breath, "except for the tan."

Mr. Richter helped his wife aboard and joined the girls on the stern of the boat. "Fishing is a serious business for these men," he explained. "They all make their living from these boats, and spend hours every day of the year fishing for tuna, mackerel, or whatever is in season. Those boats over there that look like miniature tugboats are lobster boats. And that huge boat over there with the things that look like cranes rising out of the deck? That's a shrimp boat—those men can spend up to two weeks at sea."

The girls nodded and watched as the crew used the winches to raise the heavy white nets up to dry. Suddenly J.L. let out a laugh.

"That guy over there in the plaid shorts and sombrero doesn't look too serious to me."

Jessica and Penny watched the man struggling to climb aboard a fishing boat. "Yeah, J.L.," Jessica laughed, "he looks more like an ad for bad taste!"

"You're right, Jocelyn, he definitely isn't a 'conch.'" Her father chuckled.

J.L. was growing embarrassed by her father's lecturing. "What's that?" she asked, barely able to conceal her annoyance.

"'Conch' is a term they use down here for the natives.

It looks like some of these 'conchs' make their living guiding tourists to good fishing spots. My guess is that that man's a tourist."

J.L. smiled at her father's amazing conclusion. "We could probably use a guide too, huh, Dad?"

"We'll see about that," Mr. Richter shouted as he started the motor. "Let's go!"

The three girls settled into their seats facing the sun. "Now, this is more like it," J.L. purred. "Time to start on that tan, girls. I think we should give the guys of Collingwood High a little something to gawk at when we get home." She and Penny took off their T-shirts and coated themselves with suntan oil.

"No one's going to look twice at you two bathing beauties with *me* around," Jessica joked, pointing to her baggy borrowed clothes. "Oh, well," she added to herself, "at least I won't have to impress anyone when we're out at sea." In fact, the sun was so brilliant that Jessica was relieved that her sensitive, freckled skin would be protected.

Mr. Richter eased the skiff from the dock and soon the *Dow Jones* was skipping across the waves. He squinted and surveyed the water, until he seemed satisfied with one spot and stopped the motor.

"Check out this water," Jessica said, peering over the edge of the boat. "It's so clear you can see the bottom."

"Any fish?" J.L. asked skeptically, without opening her eyes.

Penny got up and crossed to the rail. "Well, actually," she said, "there's nothing but rocks."

"All right, Dad!" J.L. teased her father.

"Come over here, girls. You too, Jocelyn," Mr. Richter called from the bow. "Let me show you something. See that ridge right there?"

The girls gazed at a formation on the bottom that resembled an enormous finely chiseled stone.

"Looks like a rock, doesn't it?" J.L.'s father continued. "But what you're really looking at is the skeleton produced by a living animal, coral."

"An animal!" Jessica stared in disbelief. "I've seen pictures of coral, but I always thought it was a plant or something!"

"Not so, Jessica. Inside, there is a living animal. And see that shadow over there?" he continued. "I'll bet you that's the shadow of a bonefish."

"Where?" Jessica shrieked, as the shadow darted behind the coral ridge and disappeared.

"Well, it's gone now, you bigmouth," said Penny. "Nice job."

Mr. Richter chuckled. "Penny's right, Jessica. Bonefish are supposedly very shy. I've heard that they are actually able to see out of the water and take off as soon as they hear a human voice. Real bonefishing enthusiasts compare it more to hunting than fishing. So the quieter we are, the better."

Mrs. Richter found four fishing rods and a tackle box in the bottom of the boat. Seeing the four of them huddled over the rail, she called cheerfully, "How's it look?"

"Hopeless," answered J.L. as she turned around. "Absolutely hopeless."

Mrs. Richter ignored her daughter's negative comments and went to join the others. "I could only find four rods," she said, "but we seem to be down to four fishermen anyway." She glanced back at J.L., who was again stretched out to the blazing sun. Mrs. Richter knew J.L. wasn't fond of fishing, and getting a tan was of prime importance.

"Well, let's see what we've got here," Mr. Richter murmured, opening the lid of the tackle box. "Bob Taylor takes this sport very seriously, so his flies should be in perfect order."

"Flies? What a relief!" Jessica commented, unable to hide her distaste for live bait.

Mr. Richter resumed his explanation. "Bonefishing is a kind of fly-fishing. See these rods? They're longer and lighter than average fishing rods."

He handed one rod to Jessica and one to Penny, chose two flies, and attached them to the girls' lines. Without wasting a second, Penny and Jessica tossed their lines into the water and began bobbing them up and down.

"No, girls! No!" Mr. Richter called. "You have to cast out!" He sighed, looking at Mrs. Richter. "It looks like I've got my work cut out for me."

Before long, the girls seemed to get the hang of it and started casting off enthusiastically. On her third attempt, Penny snapped the long pole in a move closely resembling a tennis serve and managed to hook the handle of the tackle box.

"That's our Sagittarius!" Jessica laughed loudly. "The great athlete!"

After an hour, the girls began to get distracted— no one had hooked a single fish. J.L. called to her father, "Doesn't look like the fish are biting, Dad."

"They've got something over there!" Penny shouted, shading her eyes and pointing to a boat that had been drifting in and out of view and was now only a short distance away. "In fact, now that I think of it, it seems like every time I've looked over at that boat, they were pulling in a fish. They've probably caught everything for miles."

"Mr. Richter," Jessica asked politely, "do you suppose we could ask them how they do it?"

"Well, now, Jessica," Mr. Richter answered, "there *is* a pretty strict code of privacy among fishermen. It would be improper to impose upon another boat that was having better luck."

"David, Jessica may have a point," Mrs. Richter wheedled. "That looks like a boat with a guide to me— I don't think they'd mind, and with the luck we've been having, it's certainly worth a try." She caught his eye and motioned toward the restless teenagers. J.L.'s father grinned.

"Okay, okay, I suppose it can't hurt. But let me do the talking."

"Sure thing, Mr. Richter," chimed the girls.

Mr. Richter started the motor and slowly approached the neighboring boat. As they drew near, the girls could make out two heavyset men. Suddenly J.L. leapt up and crossed to her friends at the rail, nudging Penny.

"Look at that," she gestured urgently. "Look at the name of the boat."

Jessica and Penny squinted at the bow. "*Aquarius!*" Penny exclaimed.

Jessica smiled. "That sounds like a friendly omen to me."

"Ahoy," cried Mr. Richter when the *Dow Jones* pulled alongside the older, larger *Aquarius.* "Looks like you're having better luck than we are."

One of the men on the deck, wearing an outlandish fishing hat covered with old lures, looked up with a proud smile.

"Well, if we are," he drawled, "I'd say it's thanks to our young guides." The girls quickly surveyed the deck of the *Aquarius.* Toward the bow, a deeply tanned boy who looked about thirteen was leaning against the railing, eyeing Mr. Richter cautiously.

"Guides?" Jessica joked quietly to her friends. "I only see one, and he's not even old enough to drive."

"Hmm, you're right, Jess. I wonder what he means . . ." Penny broke off and all three girls froze. The sunshine seemed to grow brighter as the young skipper rose from behind one of the men and walked toward them on the deck.

Jessica gasped, "It's the guy in the picture!"

"What picture?" J.L. asked, never removing her eyes from the tanned, blond-haired hunk.

"The one in my locker at school," Jessica sighed. "Even down to those blue eyes and gorgeous smile."

For once, J.L. and Penny didn't even seem to be listening to Jessica.

"He's ideal," Penny whispered.

"Yeah," the other two agreed. The tall young man stepped forward and nodded to J.L.'s father.

"How ya doing?" he called, a teasing note in his voice. "Fine day for fishing. Hey, isn't that Mr. Taylor's boat?"

J.L.'s father nodded.

"How's the action on the ol' *Dow Jones* today?" the captain called.

"Fabulous. Just fabulous," Jessica muttered under her breath. Penny giggled.

"Yeah, now it is," J.L. whispered.

Mr. Richter shot a glance at his daughter and her friends, then turned back to the young man, slightly embarrassed.

"Well, to tell you the truth, we haven't caught a blessed thing all afternoon." Looking toward the girls, he added, "We were getting a little frustrated, actually, watching those men hauling in fish after fish, and we thought we'd come over and find out what your secret is."

The captain of the *Aquarius* looked at the three girls

clustered along the rail and smiled obligingly.

"Hello," he called. "So you're looking for some free tips, huh?" J.L. blushed and the other girls smiled back stupidly at the "hunk." They hadn't heard a word he said.

Mrs. Richter stood up and joined her husband. "That's about the size of it." She nodded, gesturing toward the two hefty men lounging in the stern of the *Aquarius,* their plentiful catch visible in a cooler between them. "So far, it looks like we'll be eating hot dogs for dinner."

The handsome fishing guide stood listening, his head turned sideways so that his straight, sun-bleached hair was blowing across his face. When he looked up, his smile doubled in size and brilliance.

"Well, we can't have that, can we?" he said, winking at Mrs. Richter. "What do you think, Tony?" he called to the boy, who still was watching suspiciously. "Think these folks would have any luck in Pirate's Cove?"

The boy watched the captain, obviously curious about his interest in these strangers. His only answer was a slight shrug.

"I can't guarantee you anything, but if I give away a secret, you have to promise not to spread it around. Bad for business, you know. We don't normally do this," the guide added, nodding toward the boy, "but let's see if we can hook you something for dinner."

As the gorgeous blond quietly pointed out some fishing spots to Mr. Richter, the girls tried to outdo each other in looking cool and uninterested. J.L. returned to her seat and sprawled casually toward the sun, donning her sunglasses to hide her admiring eyes. Penny, leaning against the rail, undid her ponytail and shook her head a few times to fluff out her mane of blond hair. But both J.L. and Penny found it hard to keep their composure as they watched Jessica attempt to pose alluringly in her oversized clothes.

In the middle of his explanation, the skipper of the *Aquarius* glanced back at the three girls and flashed a smile. Penny pretended not to notice, and Jessica felt herself turning bright red. But J.L. felt sure she had attracted his attention. She lifted her sunglasses and regarded her friends smugly.

Those two look ridiculous, she thought. They might as well not even bother. It's obvious he was looking at me. After all, I'm acting calm, collected, and mature. Her thoughts were abruptly interrupted when a large fly landed directly on the tip of her nose. She tried to get rid of it by wiggling her nose slightly, but it stubbornly remained. Then she tried to brush it away without losing her appearance of ease. Finally her frustration got the better of her, and she sat up, flailing angrily at the persistent insect. Penny saw J.L. waving her arms wildly and burst into uncontrollable nervous laughter.

"Oh, J.L.," she howled, "we can always count on you to put things in perspective." J.L. shot Penny an angry look.

"Quick," Penny whispered to Jessica. "Let's get her out of view where she can't embarrass us anymore." The three girls moved to the opposite side of the boat, their backs to J.L.'s father and the attractive young man.

"Okay, okay," Jessica said matter-of-factly. "He's perfect. That's all there is to it. I've checked it out, and he is definitely perfect."

J.L. shrugged. "Well, I saw him first," she said to Jessica, also with a matter-of-fact tone in her voice. "And he saw me first. So I think you can just sit this one out, Jessica. Oh, and you too, Penny."

"What!" Penny exploded. J.L.'s maddening self-assurance aroused her competitive nature. "This isn't 'finders keepers,' J.L. Who cares who he looked at first? What matters is who he looked at *longest*. And I don't think there's any doubt who that was," Penny proclaimed with a vain toss of the head.

"I think he's leaving," Jessica mumbled, peering between her two companions.

"See you all later," the young man called happily to the girls. They turned, trying to attract his attention, but all they got was a friendly wave. The two men on the boat saluted J.L.'s father as they released the *Dow Jones* and the two boats began to drift apart.

"'Bye." The girls waved.

Mr. Richter started up the engine and called to the girls, "We're in business now. That young man gave me directions to a foolproof fishing spot."

But the girls didn't seem to hear J.L.'s father's optimistic words. They were lost in thought, gazing at the disappearing *Aquarius* and its gorgeous captain.

4

The sun was starting to set when Mr. Richter guided the *Dow Jones* back into the Duck Key Marina. The scene on the docks was even more lively, as the captains and crews of the dozen shrimp boats prepared for their night fishing journeys. J.L. hurried across the dock, fastening the mooring lines, while Jessica and Penny looked from boat to boat, trying to locate the *Aquarius* or spot its captain. Mrs. Richter joined them at the stern.

"Well, did you enjoy yourselves, girls?"

"You bet! I'm so glad Mr. Richter asked that fishing guide for suggestions," Jessica answered. "He really made our day—"

"What Jessica means," Penny jumped in, embarrassed, "is that if it wasn't for that advice, we would never have caught all these." She pointed to the ice chest, which now displayed six good-sized bluefish.

Mrs. Richter laughed knowingly. "I understand what Jessica means," she said, playfully tapping Jessica's glowing nose with her finger. "Looks like you got a little sun, Miss Holly."

"Oh, no," Jessica groaned, touching her nose self-consciously. "I'd give anything to tan like J.L., or like you do, Penny."

Penny smiled, pulling at her sun-streaked blond ponytail. "But, Jessica," she kidded, "you know what they say about redheads."

"I know, I know," Jessica sighed. "But why couldn't I be a redhead with a deep tan?"

"Oh, Jessica," Mrs. Richter laughed. "Come on, you two, how about a hand with these fish?"

Penny and Jessica each grabbed a handle on the ice chest and lifted it onto the dock. J.L. and her father soon joined them.

"Hungry, girls?" Mr. Richter asked playfully.

"You know, girls, J.L.'s father cooks the most spectacular fresh-fish dishes on the east coast—in my opinion, anyway," Mrs. Richter added.

"What do you think, J.L.?" Penny asked with a wink.

J.L. smiled. "I'll have to agree with Mom on that one."

J.L.'s father offered to stay behind with his wife to secure the skiff for the night. Jessica, Penny, and J.L. looked at each other, seeming to share the same thought. Without anyone's suggesting it, the three girls gathered their things and took off toward the hut at the entrance of the marina.

Standing outside the tiny weathered hut, the old dockmaster peered at the approaching girls and drew on his cigarette. As they came near, the corners of his mouth curled slightly into a greeting. "Well, hello, young ladies. Have any luck?" he asked. He exhaled the smoke, and his dark, craggy features showed no hint of friendliness. Only the deep, clear gray eyes that twinkled beneath his enormous eyebrows betrayed a gentle nature.

Penny stepped forward and answered, "We didn't catch a thing for hours, but then we got a hot tip from someone."

"A hot tip, eh?" the old man asked, narrowing his eyes and looking from Penny to J.L. to Jessica. Returning at last to Penny, he drew mightily on his cigarette and remarked, "You know, around these parts, tips aren't so easy to come by. These men hang on to their secrets like conchs to their shells."

J.L. and Jessica giggled, remembering Mr. Richter's use of the term "conch" as a description of native fishermen.

The dockmaster glanced at them and continued, "Just who gave you this little tip?—if you don't mind my asking, ladies," he added with the tiniest hint of a smile.

Penny shuffled her feet, embarrassed. "Umm—" she began, but was quickly cut off by J.L.

"Somebody on another boat, an older, bigger one called the . . . ah, the *Aqua* . . . the *Aquaman* or something like that," she said, feigning innocence.

Jessica joined in. "No, J.L., I think it was the *Aqueduct*. Or maybe not. What *was* the name of that boat?"

Penny snapped her fingers, pretending to suddenly remember. "Wasn't it the *Aquarius*, you guys?" she asked.

"That's it," they cried together.

The wise, weathered dockmaster peered again at the girls, a knowing smile spreading across his wrinkled features. "Ah, yes, the *Aquarius*. That's one of our boats, all right. Docked right over—" The dockmaster was interrupted by a voice urgently calling him from a nearby deep-sea-fishing boat.

"Bud! Hey, Bud! Can you give us a hand over here? Looks like one of the moorings pulled loose."

Bud, taking another patient pull at the tiny cigarette that remained, turned slowly toward the boat where the voice came from and nodded. The girls hardly even saw his head move, but apparently the man aboard the troubled vessel knew that he had been heard, and called back, "Thanks."

The old man returned his gaze to the girls, his face returning to its original indecipherable expression. "Excuse me, ladies. Looks like we've got a little problem over there. I hope you have—"

"What about—" Jessica began, seeing the old man starting to turn away from them as he spoke. She caught herself as J.L. and Penny wheeled on her, embarrassed.

"Real subtle, Jess," Penny whispered under her breath.

The dockmaster started off, but turned halfway back to them, pulled the cigarette from his mouth, and tossed it away. "It sure was nice of Captain Noah to give you that tip today. And I'm glad your day was successful." He turned and began to walk away, then turned back again. A faint smile again appeared around the corners of his mouth. "If, ah, if you need another tip, his boat's docked right over there. I'm sure he'd be glad to help you out again."

Bud pointed toward the farthest extension of the dock, and following his gesture, the girls finally spotted the *Aquarius*. About forty yards of water separated it from the *Dow Jones*. Noah stood on the deck with his shirt off, lounging with Tony and watching the other boats. Bud wandered away to help the man in the nearby boat, but the girls' eyes remained fixed on Noah's tanned form. Suddenly Noah crossed to the near railing and called across the water, "Hey, how was fishing in Pirate's Cove?"

The girls followed his gaze across to the *Dow Jones*, where Noah had spotted J.L.'s father. "Not bad," Mr. Richter called back, rising and nodding to the captain. The rest of the conversation was lost to the girls, but they saw Noah toss his head back in laughter and heard him say, "You're welcome."

The girls kept their eyes fixed on the *Aquarius*. J.L.'s father noticed them standing motionless at the marina's entrance. He watched them, then glanced back at the handsome young man. Grabbing an armload of fishing equipment, he started toward the girls.

"Jocelyn, Jessica, Penny, come on over and give me

a hand with this stuff," he called. The girls hadn't seen him approaching, and J.L. straightened quickly. She elbowed Jessica, who couldn't seem to tear her eyes away from the *Aquarius.*

"C'mon, Jessica, let's pitch in." The three girls reluctantly gave J.L.'s parents a hand loading the car, and even more reluctantly climbed in and left the marina.

At the end of dinner, Mr. Richter wiped his mouth and pushed back his chair. "Well, girls, was Anne right? Wasn't that some of the best fish you've ever tasted?"

"You bet," the girls chorused.

"I have to admit, it almost justifies the barbarity of fishing," J.L. conceded with a grin.

The girls rose and began to clear the table.

Mrs. Richter leaned forward with a cheerful glimmer in her blue eyes. "I tell you what, girls," she said. "I'll do these tonight if you light a nice fire for us on the beach. I think you'll find some wood around back."

"Sounds great!" Jessica declared, rising with the others and crossing to the door. J.L.'s father watched the three attractive teenagers exit, then sighed.

Mrs. Richter came up behind him and put her hands on his shoulders. "Are you thinking what I'm thinking, dear?" she asked gently.

"Well, Anne, I trust J.L. and her friends, but you saw the attention they got today at the marina. Those are three very pretty young women, and I feel responsible for them. I think we should have a little talk."

"I suppose so, David," his wife assented. "I don't think it's necessary, but it can't hurt."

Outside, the evening air was cool, and the last of the daylight made the old cottages look even more quaint. It wasn't long before the girls had built a roaring fire on the beach. Penny, Jessica, J.L., and her parents gathered around, enjoying the last of the daylight and watching the sea grow dark. Gradually the girls settled, the pounding of the gentle surf calming them into silence. In the relaxed atmosphere of the crackling driftwood, J.L. sensed that her father had something to say. She yawned and stretched, tossing her long hair.

"I'm beat." She yawned. "Bet I sleep well tonight."

Penny laughed. "No kidding. What a day! It's hard to believe we woke up this morning in Collingwood, and look at us now!"

"What about all those big parties they're giving in our honor tonight?" Jessica joked.

"Oh, darling," Penny drawled, "we can do that any night."

Jessica couldn't help laughing at Penny's acting, but Mr. Richter shifted tensely.

Uh-oh, J.L. thought to herself, and shot a warning glance at her two companions.

Mrs. Richter skillfully eased the tension. "Jocelyn," she began, "that reminds me—now that we're all together for a minute, let's go over the plans for the rest of our stay. You girls already know that Mr. Richter and I are going to visit the Pattersons on Key Largo tomorrow." Turning to Penny and Jessica, she explained, "They're old friends of ours from college. They live in a secluded area and there wouldn't be much for you to do, so we thought you all would be happier staying here."

Jessica nudged Penny discreetly.

"And then on Sunday," Mrs. Richter continued, "we think it would be fun to spend the day in Key West." J.L. smiled at her mother. She knew her parents had spent their honeymoon in Key West, and she thought it would be interesting to see the place she had heard so much about. Jessica and Penny nodded, but deep down they were both sorry that they would be away from *him* for a whole day, especially with time so precious.

J.L. jumped up when her mother finished. "Let's take a walk," she exclaimed to her friends.

"Not so fast," Mr. Richter interrupted.

"Here it comes," J.L. whispered as she sat back down in the sand. For a moment, the crackling of the fire seemed to imitate the brittle tension in the air. Finally Mr. Richter laughed.

"It's not as serious as all that," he said, gazing at the three apprehensive faces. "I just wanted to remind you of a few things we talked about today."

The girls waited restlessly.

"First of all, I just want you to keep in mind that we are all guests here, guests in a community that is the home and workplace of many people. Most of them, as you saw today, make their living from the sea." He paused for a moment and looked gravely at the three girls. "As far as ground rules for the weekend, girls, I'm not going to say more than this: I trust you, Jocelyn, and I think it's enough just to ask that the three of you use your judgment as far as what is proper and not proper behavior."

J.L. smiled. "Of course, Dad," she assured him. "You know you can trust us."

"I know, Jocelyn." He beamed proudly. He paused, then went on. "The second thing is more along the lines of a favor. This is a fishing community, and the locals have a reputation for being a rough lot. They work hard, as you've seen, and they play hard, too. They have different ways from people you're used to. For this reason, and for your own good, the town should be off limits at night."

Penny and Jessica looked at each other and squirmed slightly.

"But, Dad," J.L. began to object. "What if . . ." She broke off, realizing it was useless to argue. After all, she thought to herself, we don't really have any reason to go out alone at night anyway, and we're only going to be here two more nights.

"Okay?" Mr. Richter asked.

J.L. gave her friends an encouraging look, and together they nodded in agreement.

Mr. Richter smiled. "Now you can take that walk."

The three girls rose to their feet, being careful not to appear too eager, and walked out of the circle of firelight. They walked down the beach toward the water without speaking. A three-quarters moon shone on the rippled surface, and the high tide carried the warm waves across their feet. Jessica inhaled deeply.

"Well, that wasn't so bad." J.L. chuckled, letting out a heavy sigh when she felt safely out of her parents' hearing. "And you know, he didn't say anything about daytime activities."

"I, for one, am going to spend tomorrow at the marina," Penny announced dreamily.

"Not without me you're not," J.L. countered, and for a second the two tall girls stood still and faced each other in the moonlight.

Jessica stepped between them. "Well, both of you are going to have to contend with me, then," she proclaimed, "because when you arrive, you're going to find that I'm already lounging with Captain Noah on the deck of the *Aquarius.*"

Penny and J.L. broke their stare and laughed. Penny gave her a playful sock on the shoulder. "It looks like the race is on, then," she said.

J.L. started walking again, and her friends followed a step behind her. "The *Aquarius,*" she mused. "It's a great name for a boat."

"I'm not so sure about that," Jessica spoke up. "Aquarius is the water bearer—and I for one wouldn't want to own a boat that bore water!"

Penny bumped Jessica toward the sea. "Very funny, Jess. But you're right, J.L. Noah's sign could be Aquarius. I think it is a great idea to name a boat after your sign. Anyway, it's better than the—ahem—*Dow Jones,*" she mimicked in a deep voice.

"I wish you had your astrology book, Jessica," J.L. said. "Maybe it would tell us something about which of us would be most compatible with him. And we could read what it said about the Aquarius man!"

"I know, I know," replied Jessica apologetically. "We're not going to solve this little problem any other way, I'm afraid."

"What's the problem?" Penny asked. "I just hope you two aren't too brokenhearted when Noah falls for me tomorrow."

"Dream on, Penny," J.L. snorted. "How old do you think he is, anyway?"

"Oh, nineteen or twenty," Penny said as she turned to J.L. and innocently stated, "What do you mean, J.L.? I think it's only natural that he would pick me, the sportswoman, and incidentally the blond," she bragged, flicking her ponytail with the back of her hand. "Jessica's too short, and you're just impossible, J.L."

Jessica and J.L. glared at Penny, and Penny instantly realized she had gone too far.

"Oops," she muttered, clapping her hand over her mouth. "I didn't mean it, you guys."

J.L. and Jessica quickly calmed down. They knew

Penny too well to take her comments personally.

"Still," J.L. declared, "we'll see who he likes." "Right!" Jessica seconded. "I just wish tomorrow would get here. I can't wait to see him again." She drifted away from the others and searched the sky for the familiar constellations of the zodiac. She tried to find Virgo in the February sky, but tonight the moon was just too bright. It glimmered on the water of the ocean and shone its romantic light on the three smitten teenagers.

"I can't wait either," J.L. sighed.

5

J.L. rolled over and groped for her watch on the night table beside her. When she finally managed to focus on the tiny face, she let out a gasp and jumped up. She shook Jessica and Penny awake.

"What is it, J.L.? Is there a fire?" Jessica groaned, diving back under the covers.

"No fire, but it's after ten o'clock. I can't believe we slept so late. I thought we'd wake up with the sun."

Penny reached over her head, pulled at the curtain, and moaned in disappointment. "I have news for you, J.L., there *is* no sun today."

J.L. slumped onto the bed and shook her long brown hair in frustration. "Well, so much for our day at the marina with Captain Perfect. This always happens. Just when the vacation starts to get exciting, you end up stuck inside all day playing Scrabble."

Jessica raised up on one elbow and feigned enthusiasm. "Scrabble? Did I hear someone say Scrabble? I think it would be great to travel fifteen hundred miles on a weekend and then play Scrabble. I hope the kids in Collingwood don't hear the Florida weather. They must think we're beautiful and tan by now!"

J.L. and Penny laughed halfheartedly, but soon the three girls fell into a gloomy silence, sinking deeper into disappointment. A knock at the door aroused them.

"Good morning, girls," Mrs. Richter called cheerfully. "Are you going to sleep all day?"

J.L. dragged herself off the bed, opened the door, and let her mother in. "Oh, you're all awake already," Mrs. Richter observed. "It's so quiet in here, though. It looks like you've lost a best friend or something."

Jessica tried her best to laugh. "No, Mrs. Richter, it's just this weather. We were looking forward to a long day on the beach, and instead we get this . . . monsoon!"

"Oh, come on, you three. It's still early, and down here the weather can change in an instant. I just came in to make sure you were up and to let you know that J.L.'s father and I are leaving for the Pattersons' soon. We'll be back around five thirty. There's plenty of food in the refrigerator for lunch. We'll all go out for dinner when we get home."

She turned cheerfully to the door, then paused. "Oh, by the way, Jessica, your bag was delivered this morning, safe and sound. If these airlines would just get it right the first time, they wouldn't have to send a car all the way down from Miami. I'm glad it's here, dear.

Have some breakfast and cheer up!" She leaned back into the room and added with a wink, "I've got my fingers crossed for the weather. Have a great day, girls."

When they heard Jessica's bag had arrived, the girls' mood improved. They jumped out of their beds and hurried to the living room. Jessica quickly inspected the bag, sat down and opened it, her friends huddled around her. Mr. Richter, standing by the door waiting for his wife, watched the girls and chuckled.

"What's in there, girls?" he asked. "I didn't realize Jessica had packed anything more important than clothes."

Jessica looked up at him and was about to answer when she saw the silencing look in J.L.'s eyes. "Just that! I've got my own clothes today," she filled in quickly.

J.L.'s father smiled, satisfied with her answer. "We'll see you later, girls," he announced as Mrs. Richter joined him at the door. "The Pattersons' phone number is next to the phone."

"Okay," J.L. answered impatiently. "Have a nice time."

"Thanks for covering, Jess. You know how my father gets about astrology and the Zodiacs," J.L. explained as the sound of the car faded in the distance. The girls gathered quickly around the breakfast table. Jessica sat between J.L. and Penny, poring over her astrological guide.

"C'mon," Penny urged, "read what it says about

him." Jessica raced through the pages, reading certain phrases aloud to her friends. " '*Aquarius . . . essentially a realist . . . refusal to conform . . . frequent use of the word "friend" . . . intense flattering curiosity . . . coolly impersonal approach . . . eyes blue, likely to be blond . . .*' "

Jessica looked up at Penny and J.L. and winked delightedly. " '. . . *an obstinate way of not letting you know what he's up to . . . his mind and body must both be free as the wind.*' "

"Such a beautiful wind!" J.L. muttered under her breath. While Jessica read, Penny had been scribbling a chart on a piece of paper. She finished and groaned in disappointment.

"What's up, Penny?" Jessica asked.

"Oh, I was just arranging all the signs according to their elements—you know, the fire signs, earth signs, air and water signs. I figured that would settle which one of us would be most compatible with Noah. But it looks like it's not going to be so easy."

"Why not?" J.L. asked, apparently confident that the chart would prove that *she* was most compatible with Noah.

"Take a look," Penny offered, placing the piece of paper on the table in front of Jessica. The chart read:

FIRE	AIR	EARTH	WATER
Aries	Gemini	Taurus	Cancer
Leo	Libra	Virgo	Scorpio
Sagittarius	Aquarius	Capricorn	Pisces

"See what I mean?" Penny asked. "J.L., you're a water sign, Jessica's an earth sign, and I'm a fire sign. And Noah . . ." Penny sighed. "Noah is an air sign. That doesn't help us too much."

"Hold on a second," said Jessica, her voice growing excited. She fumbled with the book, finally producing some loose sheets of paper from inside the back cover. "That may not have helped us much, but these will!"

"What are those?" J.L. asked, leaning over and trying to read the pages.

"Compatibility charts," she answered triumphantly. "I just remembered that I stuck them in here after our last Zodiac Club meeting. Remember, I brought them to try to convince Gail to give up that boyfriend of hers?" J.L. and Penny laughed.

"Yeah, that worked great, Jess," Penny said. "And now she likes that cute guy in the band that you had your eye on."

Jessica's face turned bright red. "Well, I guess that did sort of backfire," she mumbled, slumping in her chair.

"But what about these charts, Jess? Come on, read them," J.L. urged, anxious to find out about her romantic future with the gorgeous Aquarian.

"Okay, okay. Let's see . . . Aquarius and . . . Who's first?"

"Me!" J.L. shouted. Then she glanced at her friends, embarrassed. "Um, I mean, I can wait. No hurry. Go ahead, Jessica, read Penny's first."

"That's all right, J.L.," Penny chuckled. "Be my guest. Jessica?"

Jessica quickly scanned the page. "Here goes, *'Aquarius and Scorpio: a need for respect here for lasting love.'*"

J.L.'s face took on a look of smug satisfaction and her dark eyes seemed to smolder with anticipation.

"Lasting love," she said dreamily. "How could he help but respect me, and I have nothing but respect for him."

"Nothing but *respect*, J.L.?" Jessica teased. "Respect doesn't sound very passionate to me."

"That shows how much you know about meaningful relationships, Jessica," the proud Scorpio declared. "Respect has to be there first—the passion will take care of itself."

Penny fidgeted nervously. "What about me?" she asked, nudging Jessica.

Jessica turned back to the compatibility chart and read, "*'Aquarius and Sagittarius: love is an adventure.'*"

"See that?" J.L. said sarcastically. "Everybody knows adventures are short-lived."

"That's what they think," Penny shouted angrily. "Well, whoever wrote that certainly doesn't know me!" Penny gave J.L. and Jessica a warning look. "And if you two think you do, you're wrong too. I'm up for an adventure!"

"That's Penny doing her reckless Sagittarius impression again," Jessica pretended to whisper to J.L.

Penny felt herself blushing. "What about you, Jessica?" she asked in a subdued voice.

"'*Aquarius and Virgo: solid relationship . . .*'" she began confidently. Then her voice fell. "'*. . . little passion.*'" She looked from Penny to J.L., her disappointment clear from her face. Penny and J.L. laughed.

"Well, Jessica, you've got to admit it would be a waste to have a relationship with Noah that lacked passion," Penny said. "So maybe you should just sit this one out."

Jessica wheeled on Penny, her freckled face flushed with anger. "Penny, you know as well as I do that all that stuff about Virgos being cool and unemotional isn't true for me," she blurted in a shrill voice. "I'll show Captain Noah some passion he won't forget!"

J.L. and Penny exchanged a look and burst into laughter.

"Well, I have to admit *that* was a pretty passionate display, Jessica," J.L. roared. "You sound like a line straight from *General Hospital.*"

Jessica began again. "What I mean is, I think it's too early to count anybody out yet. We all have an equal chance."

Penny sighed. "None of this makes much difference as long as the weather is lousy."

"Help me clear the table," J.L. said as she stood up and walked to the sink. But before they could get up to help, she let out a joyful shout. "The rain has stopped. Isn't that blue sky over there?"

"All right!" yelled Penny, as they began to clear the table at a whirlwind speed.

"Watch those glasses!" J.L. screeched to Penny. "Don't practice that backhand of yours in here."

"Back to Plan A," Jessica said. Soon the dishes were neatly arranged in the drying rack, and the three excited girls bounded into the bedroom. They laughed and chattered as they hurried into their bathing suits and prepared for a day at the marina.

"It's great to have my own suit," said Jessica. "Wearing your clothes made me feel even shorter than I am. It may not make me look as tall and glamorous as you guys, but at least I feel I can hold my own."

"You'd better watch it today, Jessica," Penny warned. "Your face is already bright red and your freckles are erupting."

Jessica wheeled around to Penny angrily, but the concerned expression on Penny's face calmed her instantly. She laughed. "Oh, I get it, Penny. What you mean is I'd better cover this glowing, gorgeous face, or you don't stand a chance with Noah."

The three girls walked down the beach road and turned toward the marina. Just when they caught sight of the boats in the distance, Penny stopped her companions. "Wait—we can't just go and throw ourselves at Noah like this. We should have some kind of a plan."

Jessica and J.L. became thoughtful. All at once Jessica jumped. "I've got it! You guys wait here, and

I'll go on ahead and introduce myself, then casually mention you two, too."

Penny and J.L. glared at her, until Jessica broke into her disarming freckle-faced grin.

"Why don't you just skip the talking part and tackle him," J.L. teased.

Jessica looked at the sky, feigning dreaminess. "Well, J.L., that's my backup plan, you know—just in case I can't talk him into romance."

"Listen to this!" J.L. snorted. "Jessica 'all show and no go' Holly! Go ahead, let's see what Jessica can do."

Penny turned quickly to J.L. "Listen, we can't solve anything like this. It looks to me like the only way to do this is to come up with a plan that includes all of us and gives everyone an equal chance. I'm willing to risk meeting him with both of you there too, and may the stars let him like me best!"

J.L. snorted again. "Oh yeah? You're on, Penny."

Jessica stood between her two taller friends, chagrined. "Well, I guess you're right, Penny. We should all meet him together and find out what he's like. I probably wouldn't like him anyway. You know, I generally hate gorgeous blond blue-eyed boys with gleaming smiles and taut muscles."

J.L. and Penny looked at Jessica and the tension eased. J.L. grew thoughtful. "Okay, but we still need a plan. We can't just go barging onto the dock and up to the *Aquarius* and say, 'Ahoy, *Aquarius*!' without some kind of a reason for being there. We'd look like stupid teenage tourists. We need some way of getting his attention without looking foolish."

The three walked along silently for a little while, the gears spinning in each one's head. Finally Penny spoke up. "How about this? We met him yesterday out fishing, right?"

"Right," J.L. and Jessica answered quizzically.

"And he helped us catch those fish by giving us the tip, right?"

"Right."

"Well, I think we should just approach him and thank him for the tip, and then act like we want to hire him for the afternoon to guide the three of us on a fishing trip."

Jessica laughed. "Right, Penny. But why don't we hire him for the rest of the year instead? We could say that we really want to go after some rare species of fish that only lives off the coast of Australia, and it might take a while to get there, but we don't mind. Maybe two of us would starve to death along the way," she added.

J.L. cut her off. "No, that's not a bad idea, Penny," she said grudgingly. "After all, he did see us here yesterday, and why shouldn't three young women be able to hire a fishing boat just as well as two beer-bellied men?"

"Exactly," Penny affirmed. "Now that we have a plan that will work, I hope the captain doesn't ruin it for us by not being there."

As they talked, the marina grew closer, until finally they were near enough to distinguish one boat from another. All three girls shaded their eyes and peered among the tangled masts of the fishing boats. They spotted the *Dow Jones*, moored in its familiar place. At last they made out the *Aquarius*, rising and rocking slightly on the sea swell, but the deck appeared empty.

"Well, it looks like we're not going to have much luck fishing today after all," Jessica pouted. Penny stood alongside her and sighed in agreement, but J.L. strode confidently ahead.

"Coming, you two?" she called behind her as she stepped toward the marina. "Or maybe you've got cold feet all of a sudden. No matter, I'll give him your regards."

Penny and Jessica looked at each other and rushed up alongside J.L. They marched side by side past the dockmaster's hut, not even noticing the old man sitting in a shadow chewing on his pipe. The weathered dockmaster watched the three attractive teenagers marching out onto the docks in the direction of the *Aquarius* and smiled to himself.

6 ★

The girls settled into a nervous silence as they stepped onto the first of the docks. The *Aquarius* seemed a mile away from them now, and the labyrinth of worn boards tested their nerves. Penny caught her breath.

"It's bigger than I remembered it," she murmured. "Do you suppose we'll be able to find—"

"Of course, Penny," J.L. hissed. "It's right over there. Now, shhh, be cool."

J.L. and Penny strode nonchalantly, their long legs carrying them quickly past the boats. Jessica soon found herself falling behind. "No, no," she muttered underneath her breath. "How can I look cool when I have to run to keep up with those two giants?" The three were so intent on their goal that they almost walked right past Noah, who was sitting on the dock in the shadow of a large boat with three or four other men. But Noah did not miss them.

"Well, hello there," he called, flashing his white smile as he rose to greet them. The girls turned in unison, like something from a Three Stooges movie, and stood gaping at the object of their affections. Noah took another casual, friendly step forward, while the girls tried hard to regain their composure. After what seemed like an eternity of silence, Jessica cleared her throat.

"Well, if it isn't Captain Noah . . ." she began, and caught herself suddenly. They couldn't let him know that they had pried around and found out his name, she thought. Her sunburned face turned a shade redder and she stepped behind her two friends into the safety of the shadows.

Nice job, Jessica, J.L. thought. But she smiled at Noah and said, "How's the fishing?"

"Oh, a little slow right now," he answered, smiling. He came forward, sensing that they were uncomfortable in front of the older fishermen—who seemed to have nothing better to do than to watch this scene. With a nod of his head, Noah dismissed his former companions and began to walk with the girls in the direction of the *Aquarius.*

"Well, if it wasn't for you," J.L. continued bravely, "we wouldn't have caught a thing yesterday. As it was, we had a fabulous fish dinner."

Penny shifted angrily, hearing J.L. talk as if she had enjoyed the fishing.

"Thanks again for the tip," J.L. continued. "Anyway, my friends and I really love fishing and we were wondering if . . . um, maybe you would . . . uh, like to take us out."

"Take us out fishing," Penny jumped in, in a desperate save, "in your boat . . . uh, be our guide, you know? Is this your boat here?" she asked, speaking just a little too quickly. They had reached the *Aquarius* and Noah looked up at her, grinning.

"It sure is."

When he spoke, the girls became painfully aware that they had been doing all of the talking.

"Must have cost a fortune," Jessica exclaimed. "It's a real beauty."

"Thanks!" Noah replied, looking pleased with Jessica's compliment. "Actually, I inherited it. This boat used to belong to my late uncle. He taught me everything I know about fishing and boating." Noah's eyes darkened as he gaze past his boat toward the sea.

"He must have been some kind of guy," Penny murmured.

"You're right about that," he answered, gazing warmly at Penny. His eyes seemed to be able to see directly inside her, and Penny was afraid he could see her heart jump.

J.L. took a step forward and pointed at the name painted on the stern of the boat, not about to let herself be left out of the conversation. "Was he an Aquarius?" she asked.

"No," Noah answered, cocking his head down and to one side as he had when listening to J.L.'s father the day before. For a second he seemed to be lost in the memory of his uncle, but then he looked up at J.L., his eyes still deep in concentration. "No, I'm the

Aquarius. I renamed her. You see, my uncle taught me all about the stars, too. He didn't know that much about astrology, but he navigated by the stars and believed they had some power. I think he understood quite a bit of their mysterious ways. I dabble in it a little myself," he added with a smile, and turned to climb aboard his boat.

J.L., Penny, and Jessica looked at each other and burst into an excited laughter.

"What's so funny about that?" Noah asked, a self-conscious expression clouding his finely chiseled features.

"Oh, nothing, nothing at all!" J.L. responded, still smiling broadly. "It's just such a coincidence, because you might say astrology is our passion!"

"Yeah," continued Penny. "We've all had our charts done, and even have a club back in our hometown with other enthusiasts."

Noah seemed to take an even greater interest in the girls. His eyes brightened as he sat on the deck, his strong tanned legs dangling over the white sides of the *Aquarius.* "Well, what do you know." He shook his head in amazement. The girls listened eagerly. "I'd try to guess your signs," he continued, smiling, "but I'm not that good at it. Anyway, I'm already at a disadvantage here, because you know mine. But I have a feeling you're a fire sign," he said, pointing to Penny.

"Yes," she cried, feeling flattered to have attracted his first attention.

"And you must be an earth sign," he went on, turning his inquisitive gaze quickly to Jessica. She nodded quietly, trying to hold his attention a moment longer.

"And you . . ." Noah said, looking straight at J.L. J.L. proudly met his eyes. "Well, I'm not so sure about you. We'll just have to wait and see on that one." J.L. smiled mysteriously.

"Can we come aboard?" Penny interrupted.

Noah turned to her suddenly and offered her a hand. "Of course. Sorry about that! I guess I forgot my manners." He helped Penny from the dock to the smooth deck of the skiff, and let out another apologetic laugh. "Wait a minute!" he said, turning to each of the girls. "I don't even know your names. Mine's Noah. Nice to meetcha," he added with a sincere smile.

"Noah," Penny repeated, playing innocent. She extended her hand to him. "That's a name you don't hear much. Mine's Penny."

"And I'm J.L.," J.L. proclaimed as she confidently climbed aboard the *Aquarius* and moved to shake Noah's hand. "Short for Jocelyn. Oh, and speaking of short, that's Jessica."

Jessica glared at J.L. from the dock, but Noah crossed again to the side of the boat and extended his hand to her with a laugh. "Well, good things come in small packages is what I always say." He easily lifted her onto the deck and placed his other hand on top of hers. "Well, Jessica, J.L., Penny, what brings you to Duck

Key, anyway? Going to be here awhile?"

"We're here—" all three girls began at once. They broke off and looked at each other, but when they heard Noah's winning laugh, they all relaxed.

"We're only here for a few days," Jessica sighed. "I can't believe we came all the way here just for a weekend."

"Just a weekend!" Noah exclaimed. "That's not even enough time to explore the marina, let alone the rest of Duck Key. Are you down from Miami?"

J.L. suddenly felt embarrassed in front of the hard-working fisherman. "No, actually we're from Connecticut," she said quietly.

"Connecticut! Wait, that's right, you were using the Taylor's boat yesterday. Isn't he from New York?"

"I think so," J.L. nervously affirmed. "Anyway, he's a friend of my father's, and we got a last-minute invitation from the Taylors. A week ago, I couldn't have pictured being here in my wildest dreams!" she exclaimed, warming to Noah's supportive gaze.

"You guys go to school?" Noah asked, shifting his attention to Jessica.

"Yeah, I'm afraid so—" Jessica began.

"Uh-huh. It's our first year at a junior college in our town." J.L. quickly rejoined the conversation and Jessica sighed with relief. She wasn't sure how to answer the question without giving away their true age.

"So anyway," Penny began, trying to reclaim Noah's attention, "what about that boat ride? Are we on?"

His eyes twinkling, Noah shook his head. "Sorry, I'm full up for today. Let me think, though. Yes, I have a couple hours open tomorrow morning. How about that? I'll even give you a group discount—no charge for the first hour," he added with a wink at Jessica.

The three smiling faces drooped with disappointment.

"My parents are taking us to Key West for the whole day tomorrow, so we wouldn't be able to make it," J.L. explained sadly.

Noah broke in. "Key West is a blast! You'll have a great time. Of course, it would be better if you could go without your parents, I understand that," he said to J.L. sympathetically, "but if they're paying for it, I'd definitely take advantage of it. I'm sure you've heard about the sunsets there—"

"Believe me, I've heard about the sunsets," J.L. sighed. "My parents spent part of their honeymoon in Key West, and I've heard all about it a hundred times."

"Well, what you've heard is true, I promise," Noah assured J.L. "You shouldn't miss the sunset, and the town itself is just . . . well, it's unique. Oh, and I know what you should do. You all swim, right?" he asked.

"Sure," they proclaimed, Jessica somewhat doubtfully.

"You should definitely go snorkeling, then. There's a diving shop right by the docks, and they'll give you everything you need."

"I don't know about that," Jessica said tentatively.

Noah touched her arm and assured her, "Listen, they give lessons to beginners, and I know the instructor, Tom. He's great, and I'm sure you'll like him."

The girls tried to look enthusiastic, but they were not convinced they were really up for snorkeling. Noah looked at them for a minute, as if he were trying to decide something, then seemed to make up his mind.

"So how long are y'all here for again?" he asked after a pause.

"We don't leave till Monday afternoon," Jessica answered immediately. "We don't have to be back at school until Tuesday." As she said it, her friends frowned. Only two days left!

"Great!" Noah exclaimed. "Then maybe you'd like to go to a party Sunday night. That is, unless you have other plans."

The girls were in heaven. This couldn't have worked out better if they had written the script. The stars were in their favor today!

A sudden thought clouded J.L.'s face. Surely her parents would not approve of this—and yet it seemed like the chance of a lifetime. Slowly her Scorpio determination started to surface. Oh, well, she thought, I'll figure out a way to get there somehow—if it's the last thing I do. She quickly joined her friends in their enthusiastic acceptance of the invitation.

"What kind of party is it?" Penny asked.

"Well"—Noah looked into Penny's eyes—"it's being given by some friends of mine, local guys, at a bar just up the road from here. It's a local place, nothing fancy. It's called Over the Rainbow. I think you'd have a good time."

"How should we dress?" J.L. asked, once again, trying to get back into the conversation.

Noah looked J.L. up and down. "Believe me," he sighed, "it doesn't matter. I'm sure you'll look great whatever you wear." J.L. glanced at Penny triumphantly.

"Are you sure we wouldn't feel out of place?" Jessica asked Noah nervously. "I mean, we're not local— would we be welcome?"

Penny grimaced and thought: Please, Jessica, don't make him think we're not sure that we could handle it! She shot Jessica a look, which stopped her short.

"Redheads are always welcome with my friends," Noah had already begun to answer, flashing his charming smile. "Besides, would I invite you to a party if I didn't want you to be there? You'll meet a lot of interesting people. There'll be a lot of girls—I mean *women*—there too, so you won't feel funny. It's a laid-back crowd. You're my friends, that's all they have to know. So, is it all set?"

The girls nodded furiously, flattered by Noah's obvious attention.

"Okay, then, ten o'clock at Over the Rainbow. It's real easy to find—just go straight on Fisher Street— it's just two blocks ahead."

The girls relaxed for a moment, their goal of meeting the gorgeous captain accomplished.

"What are you doing for the rest of the day?" Noah asked. "Heading to the beach, it looks like."

"You bet!" Penny replied. "We have to take *some* color back north with us."

"Be careful out there," Noah warned. "Those rays are strong."

"It's hard to be careful when you only have three days to get a prizewinning tan, but we'll try," joked J.L.

Noah rose as two men, armed with fishing gear, approached the *Aquarius*. "Well, have fun, and I'll see you tomorrow night," he said. "Right now, I have to take those two guys in the Hawaiian shirts out. Funny how all the tourists around here know the same jokes. I hope I can pretend they're funny just one more time— helps get tips, you know," he added, a warm, confidential twinkle in his eyes.

The girls climbed down from the deck of the *Aquarius*, reluctantly trading places with the tourists who had hired Noah for the afternoon.

"So long," Noah said, "and don't forget about snorkeling tomorrow."

The girls waved good-bye and watched as the tanned figure walked up the deck to the waiting men.

"We can't just stand here gawking," Jessica laughed. "We'd better hit the beach." They turned and walked casually past the same group of old sailors. This time they felt smug and accepted, and J.L. even nodded to the staring men.

They headed for the road that led to the beach. As soon as they were out of sight of the marina, the girls began to shout with excitement.

"I can't believe it, a party," shrieked Penny.

"I know," agreed Jessica. "Wait till the other Zodiacs hear about this one."

"Hold on, hold on," J.L. said, stopping short. Her face had a serious expression. "My parents aren't going to let us go to any party. Remember my father's lecture last night? He trusts our judgment, he said. In other words, no parties."

Jessica looked glum. "But, J.L.," she ventured nervously, "we can't pass this up. This guy is cuter than all the guys at Collingwood High put together."

"You're right about that," J.L. affirmed. "Still, I don't see how we can do it. We'll be in Key West all day. Who knows when we'll get back? And then what? We can't just announce that we're going to meet this handsome fishing guide at the local bar. They'll have an attack. Oh, what are we going to do?" J.L. groaned.

"Come on, J.L.," Penny jumped in, her eyes betraying her Sagittarian love of danger. "We'll just find a way to sneak out and go. We can't miss this party."

"I know," J.L. admitted. "I guess we'll have to use our own judgment on this one. And my judgment is telling me we should go and shouldn't tell my parents."

"All right, J.L.!" Jessica and Penny cheered in unison. "We're going to a party!"

"Well, I know one thing for sure," J.L. declared,

turning and starting toward the beach. "If I'm going to wear my new white shirt tomorrow night, I'd better get a tan. Let's go."

The girls chose an empty spot on the beach and settled in with their towels, lotions, sunglasses, and visors.

"Ahhh," sighed Penny. "What a vacation! Did you see how he looked at me?"

"How about what he said to me?" J.L. demanded. "I'd look great in anything."

As the three friends lay back in the sun, Jessica just murmured, "Good things come in small packages."

7

The sun was shining brightly the next morning when Mr. Richter woke the girls at an early hour. Penny stretched and groaned, then threw open the curtain. The sun was up, all right, she assured her friends, although it didn't look like it had been up for very long. J.L.'s father urged the girls to hurry. They dressed quickly, and before long the car was back on the Overseas Highway.

Once again, they found themselves on a long, spectacular bridge over the water, then on one after another of the strange islands which had grown out of the coral reef. Mrs. Richter sat in front with the map spread across her lap.

"Where are we, Mom?" J.L. asked excitedly.

"What Key is that?" asked Penny, pointing to a smaller island not connected by the highway.

"Hey, wait," Jessica chimed in, "which one did we just drive over? How many are there?"

"Hold everything," Mr. Richter shouted good-naturedly. "We can't hear ourselves think! Anne, why don't you read out the names of the Keys as we cross them?"

"Good idea, J.L.'s mother agreed. "That was Crawl Key we just crossed, this one is Fat-Deer Key, and up ahead is Vaca Key."

J.L. gulped as the car crawled across the spectacular seven-mile bridge which arched high above the sea. The reflex remained from childhood, when she had held her breath on bridges. She laughed at herself, but didn't really relax until they reached the end. Then the Keys seemed to become larger and closer together. J.L. was delighted that the car was now spending more time on land than over water.

Many of the islands seemed almost uninhabited. "It's as if Miami is a thousand miles away," Jessica exclaimed, expressing a feeling shared by everyone in the car.

"Here it comes, Key West," Mrs. Richter finally announced. Jessica, J.L., and Penny craned for a view of the approaching island. Even if Noah hadn't been so enthusiastic about Key West, they would have been excited. But the handsome captain's recommendation had a lot to do with their obvious interest. Since Noah had told them about Key West, J.L. had been thinking about a sentence she had read in a travel book she found in the bookcase at the Taylors'. *To understand the other Keys and their inhabitants, you must first understand Key West, where all the cultures meet.*

They crossed the final bridge. Mr. and Mrs. Richter exchanged brief looks, which J.L. noticed. She smiled and nudged her friends.

"Remember this place, Mom and Dad?" she teased. Her parents laughed warmly.

"Oh, a little bit," Mr. Richter joked.

"Actually," Mrs. Richter added, pointing to a crowded neighborhood as they passed it, "none of these houses were here then. This whole side of the island was a huge swamp, with a few run-down fishing shanties along the coast."

"Sounds better than this," J.L. said, watching the packed streets of houses.

"Well, sure, Jocelyn. It looks like the city covers the whole island now," her father agreed. "But I understand they've worked pretty hard to save the beautiful buildings and houses in the old section of town. It was getting pretty run-down when we were here."

As they drew near the old section, J.L.'s parents began pointing out places they remembered, but the girls had a hard time catching what they said through their delighted laughter and half-stories.

"Ah, Mallory Square," Mrs. Richter said when they parked the car. "This is where we'll be tonight. Over there on the pier is where the crowds gather to watch the sun set." Following her arm, the girls saw an open area with only a few people sitting on benches. Beyond it, a merchant ship and a yacht were docked.

J.L. noticed a visitors' center in one of the old buildings near the square. She disappeared inside, then emerged moments later. Her hands were full of maps and a dozen brochures. The more I learn about this place, the more I'll have to talk about with Noah tonight, she was thinking. She looked around for the others. Finally she saw Jessica and Penny with her father, who seemed to be pointing out buildings around the square.

"Oh, Dad, don't start with the explanations, please," J.L. said to herself, hurrying to rescue her friends from another lecture.

". . . which was falling apart when we were here," J.L. heard her father saying as she joined them. "I can't believe how beautiful it looks. After all the restoration, I barely recognize a thing!" She tried to signal Penny and Jessica, but her father saw her first.

"Ah, I see you have some information for us, Jocelyn. What does it say about these buildings?"

J.L. divided up the brochures. "Here, you guys, help me look," she said. "It'll take me forever otherwise."

The girls quickly skimmed the brochures.

"Here we go," Penny announced. "Mallory Square. It says here that this area was the center of the wrecking business during the nineteenth century. Many of these buildings were warehouses and offices which developed around the wreckers. Wreckers?" she looked up and asked.

"Oh, wreckers were—" Mr. Richter began.

"Wrecking was the business of salvaging the cargo of ships that sank on the reef," J.L. interrupted. She was really glad she'd read that guidebook now. Jessica and Penny listened with interest.

"Wow, shipwrecks!" Penny's blue eyes flashed with excitement. "So these wreckers were like pirates?" she asked hopefully.

J.L. laughed. "No, Penny, although I guess there were plenty of pirates around here. But wrecking was a real business. A boat would hit the reef, and then ten or twenty boats, each from a different wrecking company, would race to the sinking ship. The first boat there would make a deal with the captain. They'd recover what they could, bring it here, and auction it off. Right, Dad?"

"That's right, Jocelyn," Mr. Richter answered. "How did you know that?"

"A little research. Always be prepared—in the Richter tradition," she declared.

The three girls started to wander down Duvall Street, the main street of the town. Mr. and Mrs. Richter followed behind them slowly, pausing to look into shop windows.

"Look, J.L." Penny called. "Here's a map that shows a good walking tour of the old town. It starts right around here and points out all the old buildings that have been restored."

"I'd rather look at people," Jessica said, wrinkling her nose. "Check out all the cute guys!" She nodded toward an outdoor café, where several men sat around tables sipping coffee.

"Hmm, you're right, as usual, Jess," remarked Penny.

"I'm thirsty," Jessica hinted with a devious smile.

"Quiet, Jess," J.L. said, as her parents caught up with them.

"Coming?" her father asked.

"Sure. We're just reading about this building," she answered. Mr. and Mrs. Richter walked ahead, stopping to look at some paintings in a gallery. The girls continued to stare into the café and were startled when two men brushed past them on the sidewalk. The men walked down the street arm in arm. Jessica, J.L., and Penny looked at each other, and then gawked as the male couple took a table at the café.

J.L. turned away. "You guys, stop looking," she said uncomfortably.

"But do you think all those guys are—" Jessica started, interrupting herself. "What a waste! The blond one was such a hunk."

The three girls remained where they were, too curious to move on. They began to watch everyone. Penny spotted another pair of men holding hands and couldn't help giggling.

"Shhh, Penny," J.L. murmured, embarrassed. "Come on, let's go."

"What for?" Penny asked. "I could just watch people all day."

"I don't know," said J.L. glancing back toward the café. "These people . . . It kind of grosses me out."

"What does?" Jessica asked.

"These people . . . the men . . ."

Penny jumped in and spoke firmly. "It doesn't gross me out—I think people should be allowed to do whatever they want."

"I agree, Penny," Mrs. Richter said.

J.L. jumped. "Oh, Mom, we didn't see you coming. I thought you were up ahead with Dad."

"And I thought you were all looking at buildings," she teased the girls.

"Well, actually—" J.L. began self-consciously.

Mrs. Richter held up a hand to stop her. "No, listen, Jocelyn. If I had known you were people-watching, I'd have stopped in the first place."

The three girls relaxed.

"It seems so weird . . ." J.L. finally mumbled.

"What is? You mean the people?" her mother asked. J.L. nodded.

"Key West is full of fascinating and different types of people!" Mrs. Richter exclaimed. "That's why it seemed so wonderful twenty-eight years ago. There's lots to see here, but I think it is the mixture of people that has alway made Key West such a unique place."

"Was it like this then?" J.L. asked, glancing again at the café.

"You mean were there gay people here? I think there were. Of course, back then society didn't really tolerate homosexuality, so it wasn't so public. But that's one of the reasons gays come to Key West. It has a different spirit from most places."

"It sure does," Jessica agreed, looking delightedly at the passing faces.

"What do you mean, a different spirit?" Penny asked.

"More tolerant and understanding of different life-styles and of people who are outsiders in other places, I guess. You remember your father talking about conchs? You know, the natives. If you ask a conch, he'll probably tell you that he's an outsider, too, different from most Americans. This is really like a frontier town," Anne Richter continued. "You know, way out at the farthest edge of the country, and it's attractive to people who feel out of place elsewhere."

The three girls and Mrs. Richter started after Mr. Richter. After what J.L.'s Mom had said, they didn't feel embarrassed about people-watching. They began to enjoy the incredible variety passing them on the sidewalk.

"You know, it is interesting, Mom," J.L. admitted. "I guess it seems weird because we just don't have such a mixture of people in Collingwood. It's mostly families."

"It's a lucky thing we don't have more variety," Jessica laughed. "In Collingwood, we have enough problems between the Hill kids and the River kids."

"Speaking of Collingwood—" J.L. began.

"The Zodiacs!" Jessica interrupted excitedly. "We should really buy some postcards or something."

J.L. glanced at the lively redhead and rolled her eyes comically. "Now, there's an original idea. What else does a good tourist do?"

"Let's make our big purchase," Penny said as she started across the street, leaving J.L. and Jessica laughing on the sidewalk.

"Well, Mother, I guess we'll be in that shop for a little while. We'll catch up to you, okay? Let's go, Jessica, before we lose her," J.L. said. They hurried across the street to catch Penny.

"How about *this* one," Jessica asked, pulling a card out of the rack. "Wait . . . Penny, do you have a pen?"

"Sure," Penny answered. Jessica turned her back to her friends and wrote frantically on the front and back of the card. When she finished, she laughed, turned, and handed it to J.L. Penny looked over J.L.'s shoulder. The card pictured a fishing boat leaving a marina. Jessica had crossed out the name on the stern and written instead: "S.S. *Aquarius.*" On the back she had written, "Dear Mara, Cathy, Gail, Elizabeth, Abby, and Jennifer: Having a perfect time—being guided by Aquarius! See you soon, with details! Love, J.L., Penny, and Jessica."

"That's perfect!" J.L. exclaimed.

Penny agreed. "It sure is, and it will keep them guessing!"

Jessica took the card, quickly wrote in Abby Martin's address, and started toward the counter. J.L. and Penny followed.

"Twenty-five cents," the woman said with a frown.

"Do you have a stamp?" Jessica asked.

The woman set a stamp on the counter and took the change.

The girls started down the street, stopping to drop the postcard in a mailbox at the corner. They caught up with Mr. and Mrs. Richter on the next block.

"Here they are!" J.L.'s father exclaimed. "Anybody hungry?"

"Yes!" all three girls and Mrs. Richter answered enthusiastically.

"There's a place down near the docks that served mostly fishermen when we were here last. The owner went fishing every morning and served his catch at lunch. You can't get anything fresher than that."

"Sounds perfect!" the girls agreed in unison.

8

Tom, the snorkeling instructor, finished his demonstration. "Any questions?" he asked.

The eleven eager students shook their heads.

"Great!" he continued cheerfully. "If you think of anything you want to know, either about how to use the equipment or about what you will be seeing on the reef, just let me know." He relaxed and leaned against a railing. A bright smile flashed across his deeply tanned face as he surveyed his class.

"What about sharks?" an older man asked, obviously embarrassed.

"Sharks!" Penny snickered. J.L. gave her a quick poke to quiet her.

Tom turned to the man with a reassuring smile. "Sharks come in all sizes," Tom began patiently, "and all kinds. Ninety-five percent of them are terrified of humans and do their best to avoid them."

"And the other five percent?" the man asked.

Tom's smile turned playful. "The other five percent are in the movies." The group broke into laughter, and the man blushed. The instructor continued, "No, sir, I don't really mean to make light of your question. When you are swimming today, there's maybe a one-in-ten-thousand chance that you'll see even a small sand shark—they're about four feet long—but I guarantee that he, or she, won't even look twice at you. As far as being attacked," he added with an encouraging nod, "the odds on that one are about the same as our chance of being struck by a meteorite as we stand here."

Penny looked up with an exaggerated gulp. "Let's hit the water!" she pretended to urge the group. J.L. and Jessica could barely restrain their laughter.

Tom winked at the girls. "Anybody else?" he asked the group.

Jessica wished she could ask Tom if he knew of any quick cures for her anxiety when it came to the water. It wasn't that she couldn't swim—her parents had made sure she learned, by practically dragging her to swimming lessons for five straight years. But even though she knew she could swim over a mile without stopping, she had never completely overcome the fear. They had combed the docks to find Tom, the instructor Noah had recommended to them. She wasn't going to ruin this vacation with her silly fears. Jessica glanced at her two friends, who were both smiling confidently at the handsome instructor. Jessica swallowed the lump in her throat and prepared for the challenge.

"Okay, let's do it!" Tom exclaimed. The students gathered up their rented masks, fins and snorkels and were led toward the dock.

The girls were the first ones to climb onto the launch Tom used to ferry divers and swimmers out to the reef, and they took a place in the stern near the motor. Tom helped some of the other students aboard, then took his place next to Penny. He started the motor and guided the boat away from the dock.

The launch skipped across the small waves toward the reef, which was a visible colorful band under the water in the distance. They could see that three or four boats were already anchored there. When they got close enough, they watched with amusement as the swimmers splashed back and forth, facedown in the water. The black tubes of their snorkels looked like tiny periscopes peeking out of the sea.

Tom cut the motor and the launch drifted for several yards before coming to a stop just at the edge of the reef. J.L., Penny, and Jessica peered over the side of the boat. The bottom, a rocky, jagged surface of coral, looked close enough to touch.

"Okay," Tom addressed his crew of students. "Before you all dive in, let me just remind you of a few things, and then I promise I'll stop sounding so formal and boring." He smiled broadly at his attentive audience. "We're now floating above the only coral reef in the continental United States. As you can see, you won't be alone out here—which means that you are just a few of the thousands of adventurous people who visit this natural wonder every year. You came because you admire natural beauty. Do *not* try to take it home with you. Souvenir hunters have already damaged much of the reef, breaking off and collecting chunks of the coral skeleton. You'll be able to see what I mean if you dive and look at it up close. It takes generations of coral to build a reef like this one, thousands of years. Please remember that."

The eleven passengers nodded.

"Now, a few things to watch for," the dark-eyed instructor continued. "All of the species of coral and fish are identified in the guides you were given on the dock. Just remember: don't touch the coral—it can be very sharp. And if you meet up with a barracuda, the only truly mean inhabitant of the reef, don't challenge him and he won't challenge you. There," Tom sighed as he finished his speech and rose to his feet. "Done. Right now, I'm sure you would much rather be seeing the real thing than listening to me gab about it."

"On the contrary," Jessica muttered, watching the tanned instructor help an older couple adjust their masks and enter the water. Ignoring her, J.L. and Penny rushed to put on their fins and masks, and flopped toward the side of the boat.

"Coming, Jess?" they called. Jessica reluctantly donned the awkward fins and shuffled over to her friends.

"Too bad Elizabeth isn't here, she'd love this," Jessica said, trying to laugh off her nervousness. When that didn't work, she turned to her friends. "This is the only part of this vacation I'd trade with our Pisces friend. Stick close to me, you two," she said timidly.

J.L. and Penny jumped enthusiastically over the side and swam a short distance from the boat. Jessica sighed and eased herself down the rope ladder into the warm, clear water. She looked up and saw Tom watching her.

"Coming?" she called, trying to hide her fear.

"No," Tom laughed. "I've been out twice already today. I'll be watching from the boat. But have fun, Jessica." Jessica was pleased that Noah's friend remembered her name. She waved and bravely pushed off from the ladder, attempting to put thoughts of barracudas from her mind.

She started kicking in the direction of Penny and J.L. At first she kicked too hard, forgetting the fins, and soon she was breathing heavily. Her breath sounded like a gale as it passed through the snorkel and echoed in her mask. With the mask, she could see every detail of the sea bottom, but she concentrated instead on the long legs of her friends treading water ahead. She reached Penny first. Penny tapped her shoulder. Jessica lifted her head out of the water.

"Jess, relax," Penny said in a soothing voice. "You're working way too hard. Kick easy! We'll be right beside you now."

Jessica caught her breath, bit into the mouthpiece of the snorkel, and lowered her head again. Following Penny's advice, she soon found herself effortlessly gliding across the reef. The three girls swam side by side.

They communicated silently, pointing at things near them in the water. There were so many kinds and colors of coral, some like patterned stone, some like elaborate fuzzy antlers, and some that resembled long human fingers. Coral fans danced gracefully to the rhythms of the ocean's currents. Jessica saw the first fish, an ugly, colorless lunker loafing on the bottom. But by the time they turned back toward the boat, they had seen too many kinds of fish to remember— beautiful gold, black, silver, and red ones—exotic- looking fish that darted ahead of them, sometimes alone, sometimes whole schools of them. Jessica relaxed so completely in this underwater paradise that she even dived a few times with her adventurous friends.

They were the first to return to the boat, and Tom leaned over the side to meet them.

"You've still got some time, you know," he told the girls.

"Thanks, but we're pretty tired," Penny said, climb- ing the ladder.

"How was it?" Tom asked brightly as he helped Jessica and J.L. aboard.

"Fantastic!" Jessica beamed. "I admit I was a little nervous, but I'm so glad Noah recommended that we do this!" They dried off and sat back on the deck, facing the sun.

"Are you friends of Noah's?" Tom asked. The girls exchanged a quick proud look.

"Well, yes, I suppose," J.L. started. "I mean, we

only really met him yesterday at the marina—"

"What were you doing up there in Duck Key? It's pretty much all conchs up there, and not too many tourists—not that you're typical tourists," he added with a flattering smile.

J.L. felt herself blush, but went on. "A friend of my father's owns a fishing cottage there, and at the last minute he and his family couldn't come, so . . ."

"So here you are. That's great!" said Tom.

"Yeah. And we met Noah fishing yesterday," Jessica jumped in.

"Was he your guide?"

"No, not really. We just sort of ran into him at sea, you know?" Tom looked puzzled, but Jessica didn't bother to explain herself. "When we told him that we were coming to Key West today, he said we had to try snorkeling, and recommended you."

Tom laughed. "Yeah, Noah's like a billboard that advertises for me up there. But he usually sends me his fishing clients—you know, the big guys who look like small islands floating in the water?"

The girls laughed wildly. "We saw him with a few of them yesterday."

"Tom, how do you and Noah know each other?" Penny asked when they had recovered.

"Well, Noah is friends with just about everyone south of Miami," Tom said admiringly, and smiled. "No, but really, he and I went to grade school together. He used to live here in Key West, and we hung around together a lot. My parents love him, because Noah would always try to speak Spanish with them."

"Spanish?" they all asked at once.

"*Sí, son cubanos*—they're Cubans. They came here from Cuba when I was a baby."

Jessica nudged J.L. and smiled. Not only was Noah gorgeous and fascinating, but his friends were too! "Why did he move?" she finally asked.

"Huh? Oh, Noah. Well, he had an uncle who lived in Duck Key—"

"The uncle with the boat!" Jessica cried, remembering Noah's story of how he got the *Aquarius*.

"Exactly," Tom said, obviously impressed.

"Are you going to the party tonight?" J.L. asked.

"Party? Oh, that's right. Noah told me about something at Over the Rainbow. I wasn't planning to, but I may change my mind," he said, a wide smile crossing his face.

Their conversation was cut short when Tom's other students began to return to the launch. One by one they climbed aboard, and before long Tom's boat was heading back toward the Key West docks.

"Let's wait until the others leave, so we can thank him," J.L. suggested as they reached the docks and Tom hustled to attach the mooring lines. Penny and Jessica agreed without hesitation. They watched Tom saying good-bye to his other students, and as he started toward his boat, Jessica stepped forward and extended her hand.

"Thanks for everything, Tom," she said. "I feel great."

"Yeah," Penny added, laughing. "My legs feel like I just played two sets of tennis."

J.L. smiled at Tom. "Really, it has been great. We hope we see you later tonight."

"Wow, this is getting better by the minute," Jessica said to the other two as they headed toward the center of town.

The three girls and J.L.'s parents wandered back to town and down to Mallory Square. A crowd had already started gathering on the pier for Key West's nightly ritual, the sunset. But spending the afternoon with Noah's friend had just increased the girls' excitement over the party. At the first opportunity, J.L. steered her two friends away from her parents.

"I'm going nuts!" J.L. confided to her friends. Penny and Jessica turned to her, surprised.

"You look sane as ever to me, J.L.," Jessica commented.

"No, I can't stand this. I mean, Key West is great, but I'm so excited about the party tonight I can't even keep my mind on it anymore."

Penny nodded in agreement. "I know, J.L. I just wish the sun would hurry up and set, so we can get going."

J.L.'s face darkened. "Now my Dad is talking about having dinner here in Key West—"

"No!" Jessica interrupted. "I can't keep Noah waiting like that!" Penny and J.L. regarded her without much sympathy.

"Jessica can't keep Noah waiting," Penny mimicked. She tossed her head arrogantly. "Forget it, Jess. It's not you he'll be waiting for." Jessica felt her face flush.

"Knock it off, you two," J.L. snapped, clearly annoyed.

"Oh, I suppose you're going to tell us that Noah is all yours?" Penny taunted J.L. The tall Scorpio turned to her, clearly insulted.

"Oh-oh," Jessica muttered.

Penny shuffled her feet and stared into J.L.'s dark, gloomy eyes. "I'm sorry, J.L. I didn't really mean anything. I guess I'm pretty nervous about tonight, and I lost my temper."

A slight smile softened J.L.'s features, and her eyes brightened. Jessica let out an exaggerated sigh of relief.

"Whew! I thought I was about to witness a Scorpio-Sagittarius storm," she said teasingly.

J.L.'s face quickly became serious again. "What we have to do is convince my father that we're too tired to stay here for dinner. Let's suggest we grab a quick sandwich and head back to Duck Key."

"Right now?" Penny asked.

"As soon as the sun sets," J.L. said. "After all, Noah did say we should check out the sunset here." When J.L. mentioned the sunset, Jessica and Penny suddenly looked around the pier, startled. They had been so preoccupied in their thoughts of Noah, they hadn't even noticed what was happening around them.

The pier had taken on the atmosphere of a free-wheeling carnival. Groups of street performers began their acts, vying for the attention of the visitors. A large circle had formed around a juggler who worked first with clubs, then knives, then flaming torches. A tall, skinny man in a tailcoat and high hat miraculously maneuvered a unicycle around the crowds of people. In the other direction, the girls could see the fading sunlight glimmering on the surface of the water. The pier was so crowded with photographers that the sound of camera shutters competed with the shrill calls of seagulls. And then almost everything was drowned out when a man and a woman started thumping out songs nearby on a guitar and a steel drum.

In the middle of all this excitement it was impossible to concentrate on just Noah. The sun dropped lower and lower and was transformed into a giant red ball sending out pink, orange, and lavender spurs. Abandoning their conversation for the moment, Jessica, J.L., and Penny squeezed to the pier's edge to find a spot with a clear view of the water.

"Noah was right, this is unbelievable," Jessica sighed.

"No kidding. It's beautiful!" Penny marveled.

As the magical moment approached, the crowd grew quieter. For a moment, the brilliant ball seemed to hover on the horizon. Then, all at once, it passed beneath the ocean's edge. The sun vanished, but left a sky aflame with color. Cameras clicked wildly. Loud cheers and applause rose from the crowd. The three girls stood mesmerized on the pier's edge until the dramatic colors began to fade and the sky darkened to gray.

J.L. nudged her friends. "Okay, enough of that," she said. "Time to get going." She led her friends through the crowd, quickly locating her parents.

"Fantastic, wasn't it!" J.L.'s father exclaimed, still shooting pictures in the fading light. "That's one thing around here they can't change."

"Dad, it's too dark for pictures," J.L. said dryly.

"Oh. Yes, so it is," Mr. Richter replied. "Well, how about some dinner?"

"To tell you the truth, Dad, I'm beat," J.L. said, winking at her friends confidentially. "Can we just get a quick hamburger and head back to Duck Key?"

"Good idea," Penny chimed in. "I'm not even sure I'll be able to stay awake on the ride home."

Mr. Richter looked inquisitively at the three girls for a moment, and then at his wife. "Not a bad idea, Jocelyn. I have to admit I feel rather tired myself."

9

J.L. woke up when she heard the sound of gravel under the tires and felt the car stop. She slowly became aware of her parents whispering in the front seat. It reminded her of when she was little and she and her brothers would fall asleep on the way home from some family party or dinner.

Why am I thinking about that? J.L. demanded of herself. I won't feel guilty about our plans for tonight. Sure I love my parents, but it's not so terrible for us to want to go out. Penny, Jessica, and I can take care of ourselves. J.L. glanced at her friends. Penny and Jess had actually fallen asleep. They were trying to rouse themselves as Mr. Richter stopped the car. The three girls tumbled out, stretching and yawning.

"Oh boy!" Jessica yawned. "I really fell asleep! All that walking and the snorkeling knocked me out."

"You're not the only one," Penny muttered. Then suddenly she added in a horrified whisper, "To think that we could have actually slept through the party! We'd better wake up fast!"

"Penny, careful," J.L. warned.

Mr. Richter watched the girls stretching and rubbing their eyes. "You three look like I feel." He chuckled. "I think it's going to be early to bed for everyone tonight. We have a big trip ahead of us tomorrow." The girls smiled sleepily.

"You're so right, Mr. Richter," Penny agreed. "This sure was a long day. But it was great!"

"Yes, thank you so much," Jessica chimed in. "It was super." J.L. rolled her eyes at her friends. They remembered their manners at the strangest times, she thought to herself.

As they began to wake up, the girls grew more and more excited. In fact, they could hardly stand still as J.L.'s parents headed toward the house.

J.L. called to her parents. "We'll be in soon. We're just going to take a short walk on the beach."

"Okay, kids," mumbled Mrs. Richter as she and her husband walked arm in arm up to the cottage, "take your time."

The girls turned and hurried toward the beach.

"I didn't think I was that tired," J.L. said, glancing over her shoulder to make sure her parents were inside the house.

"It was a great idea to come out here," Jessica said admiringly. "We have to finalize our plans for the great escape. What time is it, anyway?"

Penny checked her watch. "Seven forty-five," she said with a catch in her voice.

"And we told Noah we'd be at the party at ten o'clock, right?" asked Jessica, trying to sound calm.

"That gives us an hour and forty-five . . . no, two hours and . . . no . . ."

She began to giggle helplessly and plopped down on the sand. J.L. and Penny stopped and watched her with their hands on their hips.

"I'm so *nervous!*" Jessica admitted finally.

"Come on, Jess," Penny whined. "Let's please try to act our age tonight, okay? Please? Just this once?"

"If we did that, they wouldn't let us into the party. We're going to have to act twice our age," Jessica retorted.

"Well, I've got to admit I'm nervous too," J.L. joined in. Jessica and Penny stared at her, amazed. On the outside, J.L. looked cool as ever. "But we've got to remember, no giggle fits once we get to the party. I don't think they'd go over too well." She helped Jessica to her feet and they continued walking.

"I don't think Noah would have invited us if he thought we were too young," J.L. continued, trying to convince herself as well as the others.

"That does bring up a question," Penny groaned as she sat on a large rock and drew her knees up to her chest. "How old should we say we are?"

"Oh, Pen, you're right! Well, I guess we should all be the same age, since Noah knows we've been in the same classes. How about nineteen?" J.L. suggested. "That's not so outrageous. Are we agreed on that one?"

The others nodded. "But what if they check IDs?" Jessica asked.

"We'll worry about that after we get there," J.L. answered.

Penny gazed moodily at the ocean. She picked up a small stone and lobbed it toward the water and sighed. "You know, J.L., none of this matters unless we can figure out a way to get out of the house tonight. If your father could hear the way we're talking, he'd probably hit the roof."

"Tell me about it!" cried J.L., her confidence quickly disappearing. "And he'd be sure to let your folks know, too."

Jessica gulped. "I'll be grounded for my whole senior year, without parole," she piped up. The girls laughed nervously, but suddenly Jessica became very serious. "But it sounded like your parents were pretty tired tonight. Maybe they won't even notice."

"I don't know," J.L. said, squinting her eyes. "My mom's a pretty light sleeper." She paused and sighed in frustration. "It's going to be so much harder to sneak out here, though. At home I know where every creaky board is. I can practically float up and down the stairs without my parents hearing a thing." Jessica and Penny laughed.

"Oh, no!" Penny groaned, puffing out her cheeks. "I can do the same thing in my house. That talent alone has been responsible for zillions of late-night calories. All those two-A.M. kitchen raids!"

"You too? I always wondered if my parents ever knew about me." J.L. smiled.

"My mother never seems to catch on," Jessica joked. "She always blames it on my brothers."

The girls laughed nervously, but finally grew more serious. "But I think we could get in a lot more trouble with this little adventure. What are we going to do?" J.L. asked her friends.

"I've got it!" Jessica exclaimed. "We'll get all dressed and ready—very quietly, you know, when they think we're getting ready for bed. And then we'll get into bed and pretend we're sleeping until we're sure your parents have gone upstairs and are asleep."

"How long do you think that will be?" Penny asked, not relishing the idea of putting on her neatly ironed clothes and then lying in bed in them.

Jessica thought a minute and then decided, "Well, we'll wait at least an hour. And after an hour, one of us—J.L., I guess it should be you—you tiptoe upstairs and listen at their door. If it sounds like they're asleep, you know, snoring or something, then we grab our shoes and go." As she spoke, her nerves made her begin to get carried away with the devious plot. She talked faster. "Okay, okay, then while J.L.'s checking on her parents, we make shapes in the beds with pillows so it looks like we're still there, in case anyone checks on us—"

"You mean like the prison guards," Penny interrupted with a smile. Jessica ignored her.

"—to make it look like we're still there," she repeated. "Then we put away all traces of clothes and makeup, and we open the window a crack in case we get locked out. Oh, and no perfume—they might smell it and get suspicious. And we shouldn't—"

"Enough, Jess!" J.L. demanded. "It's not a bad plan, but let's not get out of hand. How would we ever get locked out? And why worry about the perfume? It's the smell of cigarette smoke and beer that'll be in our clothes when we get home from the bar that worries me."

"Yeah, Jess," Penny joined in the teasing, "and what will we do in the event of a tidal wave or a nuclear attack?"

Jessica fell silent, embarrassed. "Well, we do need a plan. You guys said so yourselves," she muttered defensively.

J.L. spoke soothingly. "Right, Jessica. And your idea is basically a good one. We go in, act like we're asleep—but instead, we get dressed. And then we just sneak out the front door when they're asleep. It really is lucky that we got the downstairs bedroom. It'll make for a pretty easy getaway."

In the moonlight, Penny's bright blue eyes glimmered with excitement. "You guys, I love this. It's so . . . so challenging. I'd make a great spy!"

"Yeah." Jessica grinned at the athletic Sagittarius. "Dishonesty really becomes you, Miss Ross. Or is that perhaps love I see in your eyes?"

"Love?" cried Penny. "You should talk! I saw the way you looked at him yesterday. And after you fell asleep in the car just now, you kept saying his name: 'Noah, Noah, Noah . . .'"

J.L. screeched with laughter as Penny continued, "I had to explain to Mr. and Mrs. Richter that you were dreaming the bogeyman was chasing you and you were saying, 'No, no, no'."

"Very funny," Jessica snarled back. "And what about you, J.L.? Wanting to buy those rainbow earrings in Key West? You know, rainbow-Aquarius?"

"Yeah," Penny joined in as the target of the teasing shifted. "Or what about when she asked her father if the dolphins we saw jumping around when we were driving were the same kind as the trained ones in the 'aquarius' back home!"

Jessica was holding her sides from laughing so hard. She imitated Mr. Richter's deep voice. "Don't you mean 'aquarium,' dear?"

"Hey, I was tired," J.L. started to defend herself. But she realized it was useless. "I guess we were all a little preoccupied today," she laughed. "Hey, it's getting late. I think we'd better head back to the house."

When they reached the house, J.L. took a deep breath. "Synchronize your watches, fellows—here we go!" Each one glanced quickly at the kitchen clock.

Eight thirty, thought Jessica. How will I ever be able to wait until ten? The worn screen door slammed shut behind the girls, and Mr. Richter was startled out of his doze in the easy chair.

Oh no, thought J.L. I'll have to remember that

slamming door when we leave here tonight. Mr. Richter blinked several times as if trying to focus on the girls.

"Oh, hello," he said self-consciously. "I just can't seem to keep myself awake. I heard you all giggling out there a minute ago. I just don't know where you girls get your energy," he added, shaking his head. The girls suddenly remembered that they should be acting sleepier than they were. Jessica and Penny both started to yawn at once, then stopped at the same time. Mr. Richter apparently didn't notice. "J.L., your mother already went to bed, but she asked me to say good night to all of you for her. I'm going up to bed now, too. You three can stay up for a while if you want to. There's plenty of food in the refrigerator if you're hungry. Eat up, because we can't take it with us tomorrow."

"Thanks, Dad," J.L. said, leaning over to kiss her father good night. She added wearily, "Actually we are pretty exhausted too, especially after that walk. I think we'll go to bed soon."

"I happen to think that's a very good idea. Sleep well, Penny, Jessica, Jocelyn," he said, getting to his feet.

"Good night, Mr. Richter," called Penny and Jessica. "And thanks again for a great day."

As soon as Mr. Richter had trudged up the stairs and around the corner to the bedroom, the girls sprang into action. They ran into their own bedroom, breathless with excitement. Without a word, the girls launched into their plan. They worked as if they had rehearsed it a hundred times. Bags came out from the closet and from under the beds. Makeup and hairbrushes seemed to appear and multiply like magic. All three faces were set in the same serious, determined expression.

They listened to the sound of footsteps on the floor above them, picturing Mr. Richter's movements in their minds. That was Mr. Richter walking to the bathroom, that's him walking back. Now he's walking over to the window, he opens it, yes, now he's crossing to the bed. Now he sat down. They heard the sound of one shoe dropping on the floor, and then, finally the other. All sounds from upstairs stopped.

J.L. breathed a sigh of relief. "Still no talk," she whispered. "We want them to think we've gone straight to sleep. My mother won't sleep soundly until she thinks we're settled." After what seemed like an eternity of silence, J.L. listened again. "Okay," she proclaimed at last, "now we can get dressed."

"What are we going to wear?" Jessica asked Penny in a careful whisper.

"I'm not sure. Nothing too fancy, I guess. Noah said casual, didn't he? All of a sudden everything I own looks so young."

"How about you, J.L., what are you going to wear?" Jessica whispered. J.L. raised her finger to her lips, and then, without speaking, held up a black denim miniskirt and a T-shirt stenciled with a wild, colorful abstract design. "What do you think?" she whispered.

Jessica and Penny nodded enthusiastically. Jessica picked a few things out of her suitcase and began to undress. As she lifted up her shirt, she heard Penny gasp.

"What is it?" she asked faintly.

"Your sunburn! Don't you feel it?" Penny answered. "Take a look in the mirror." Jessica walked slowly over to the mirror, hardly daring to look at herself.

"Oh, hell," she muttered. "It must have happened while we were snorkeling. I should know better than to spend that much time in the sun. It doesn't feel so bad, but I look like a boiled lobster." She slumped onto the bed.

"Here, let me help you put some lotion on it," offered J.L. "Don't worry, Jess. I'm sure it will be much better in the morning."

"Morning," groaned Jessica. "Who cares about the morning? Tonight is all that matters."

"Take it easy, Jessica," Penny comforted her. "Most of the really scorched part will be covered anyway. And I'll put makeup on your face so you'll look more tanned than burned."

"Thanks, Penny," Jessica said gratefully.

"I'm going for the preppy look tonight," Penny decided. Out of her bag she pulled a pink oxford shirt and white linen shorts. "These'll look all right together, won't they?" she asked. "With my docksiders to complete the picture."

Jessica had finally settled on a violet sweatshirt torn at the neck, the way they wore them in New York, and her favorite mid-calf black jeans. She carefully placed her black flats by the door.

J.L. was already dressed and was examining herself in the mirror from every possible angle. "I sure hope this doesn't wrinkle," she said. "If you're all ready, I guess we'd better get under the covers now."

"I'd better not put my shorts on yet," Penny complained. "They'll wrinkle like crazy. What time is it, anyway?"

"You're the one with the watch," Jessica reminded her.

"Nine forty-five!" Penny announced.

"It's almost time," J.L. said excitedly. "I don't think we'll need to get in bed after all."

"I guess we did overplan just a little bit," admitted Jessica as she hurriedly ran the brush through her hair again. "But I'm glad there isn't a whole lot of extra time. I don't think I can handle it."

The girls fell silent as they concentrated on their finishing touches.

"How about it?" J.L. asked in a whisper. "Is everyone ready?" Penny and Jessica nodded. "Then let's go. You two go first, and I'll close up behind us here."

The girls tiptoed out of the bedroom, carrying their shoes in their hands. J.L. took one final look around the room. It looked like a hurricane had hit it. But there wasn't any time to straighten up now, she realized. She'd just have to hope her mother didn't decide to check on them. And what were the odds on that? Her parents hadn't checked up on her in years, she assured herself.

Penny and Jessica waited for J.L. in the living room. She caught up with them, and the three girls stepped toward the door, carefully avoiding the furniture in the dark. No one breathed. *I can't believe how graceful Jessica is being,* J.L. thought to herself. *I was sure she'd knock something over.*

J.L. opened the front door and held it firmly as Penny and Jessica walked outside. She was just about to close it when Penny suddenly wheeled and started back inside.

"What are you doing?" J.L. cried.

"I forgot my pocketbook," Penny whispered back, brushing past J.L.

J.L. gently closed the screen door and she and Jessica stood nervously on the porch. But Penny was back in a few seconds. Before J.L. could stop her, Penny burst through the door, allowing it to slam loudly behind her. To the girls, it sounded louder than a firecracker. They froze, staring at each other. And then without realizing it, they were running down the driveway and up the street, in the direction of town.

It wasn't until they had passed four or five more houses that they dared to slow down. J.L. stopped and looked back toward their cottage. No lights had gone on upstairs. She turned to her companions.

"We did it!" she cried. Then she turned to Penny and narrowed her dark eyes. "Nice job, you clumsy oaf. You could have gotten us caught!"

"I'm sorry. I didn't know it would happen."

But J.L. continued in a huff. "When I think about what could have happened . . ."

"J.L., I already said I was sorry. You know I didn't do it on purpose," Penny protested.

Jessica coughed nervously. "Look, we made it in one piece," she assured J.L. and Penny. "Let's just thank our lucky stars and concentrate on the matter at hand—the *party!*"

Penny and J.L. nodded in agreement, slightly ashamed of themselves for bickering. The three girls started off for the bar. They walked along quietly. The moon was behind the clouds, and it was hard to make out anything of their surroundings. Occasionally they spotted small houses here and there among the whispering palms.

"It's awfully dark," Jessica whispered. "Don't they have streetlights down here?"

"I guess not. I sort of wish I had a flashlight. But then again, I guess we'd look pretty stupid walking into a party with a flashlight," J.L. answered nervously.

The streets were quiet. Unconsciously they drew closer together, as if for protection.

"How far is this place?" Jessica asked timidly.

J.L. looked around her, trying to confirm their location. "I think it's only about three more blocks," she mumbled. She was having second thoughts about this whole thing. This walk was giving her the creeps.

"I wish Abby were here," Jessica said faintly. "She's always so confident."

The closer they got to the neighborhood of the bar, the smaller and darker the cottages looked. From what they could see, many of them weren't painted, and one or two seemed to be leaning dangerously to one side. At last they turned onto a large street, and in the distance the girls could see the colorful flashing neon sign arching over the door.

"That must be it," Penny exclaimed, relieved. "Over the Rainbow."

"I'm scared," admitted Jessica. "Do you guys really want to go through with this?"

J.L. and Penny just looked at each other and sighed. In spite of her own second thoughts, J.L.'s proud Scorpio nature would never allow her to let these feelings show now. "C'mon, Jessica," she commanded, steering her down the street by her shoulders.

As they neared the bar, Penny said haltingly, "It's not very nice, is it?" The girls could hear loud laughter coming from inside. They looked at each other with a mixture of apprehension and excitement.

"This is definitely the place," Penny affirmed. Music and voices spilled out the door. A record was playing, but it was a song the girls did not recognize. Penny, J.L., and Jessica walked up to the door. J.L. barely had time to whisper, "Look confident," before a brawny, rough-looking man in his late twenties brushed past them rudely on his way out.

The girls moved closer together and peered in the door. The bar was packed full of people who seemed older than they had expected.

"Do you see him?" Penny whispered.

"No," J.L. answered. "No, I don't, but he had better be here."

The three friends took a deep breath and plunged into Over the Rainbow.

10

Inside, J.L., Jessica, and Penny were overwhelmed by the noise and smoke. The throbbing bass beat of the music shook the floor. The three girls stood for a moment near the door, craning to see through the crowd of young people standing elbow to elbow in front of them. Jessica put a hand on each of her friends' shoulders and pulled herself up onto her toes.

"What is this, the land of the giants?" she shouted into J.L.'s ear. J.L. smiled at Jessica and gestured toward Penny.

Jessica shook her head helplessly and yelled, "What?"

J.L. raised her voice so she could be heard easily over the music. "I said I can't see a thing either, but it looks like Penny has her eyes on something fascinating."

Penny turned around to defend herself, embarrassed by J.L.'s remark. But when she saw the curious smiles on her friends' faces, her expression softened.

"I see some good prospects," she said, "but no Noah."

"Good prospects!" exclaimed Jessica. The rest of what she said was drowned out. The girls retreated toward the doorway to be able to talk.

"Good prospects! You mean you'd take a chance with one of these guys?" Jessica repeated.

The girls peered through the smoke at the tight circles of young men and women, most of whom were laughing and drinking noisily. A few looked up and nodded in their direction.

"Well," Penny reconsidered, "maybe not. But they're sure okay to look at."

"Everyone here is years older than we are," J.L. whispered. "Even if we pretend we're nineteen, they'll still think that's young."

"True," answered Jessica, "but we can't say we're older than that. No one would ever believe us. I doubt they'll even believe I'm nineteen. Oh, I just hope nobody asks me anything."

"Relax, Jessica," Penny asserted. "Just act natural and self-assured. If we act like we belong, people will just assume we do."

"You sound as if you're trying to convince yourself, Penny," J.L. laughed. "I wish there was more room here, though. It looks like wall-to-wall people from here to the other side. I don't know how we're going to find Noah." The music stopped, but J.L. continued loudly, "If we could just find somewhere to sit—"

"Looking for a place to sit?" a voice broke in behind the girls. All three jumped. They turned toward the voice and tried to regain their composure.

J.L. recovered. "As a matter of fact, we could use a place to sit down and have a drink. Are there any tables here?" she asked smoothly.

The young man eyed each girl aggressively. "Yeah, sure, they have tables over there, but they're full by now. There's room for one in my car, though."

Thinking he was joking, Penny broke into loud, nervous laughter. The boy's face became angry.

"Hey, who are you?" he asked in a way that sounded more rude than interested. "I haven't ever seen you around here before."

Jessica began to fidget uncomfortably. J.L. managed a smile and said, "We're here to meet a friend. And I think we'll go look for him right now," she added, taking Jessica authoritatively by the arm. The two girls started weaving their way through the crowd. Penny looked nervously at the young man, then took off after her friends.

After what seemed like an hour and a thousand "Excuse-mes" the three teenagers broke through the last group of standing drinkers. In front of them, raised slightly above the rest of the floor, was a small area where there were several tables. J.L. nodded confidently at her friends. "Not bad, huh?"

Penny smiled. "Okay, not bad, J.L. But that guy was right about one thing. There sure isn't any room at these tables."

Jessica leaned against the wall and took a deep breath. The air was still very smoky, but at least they could see more than a few feet in any direction.

"You know, Penny, you might have been right about these guys. Some of them are pretty cute." Jessica giggled.

J.L. addressed her haughtily. "Well, Jessica, you can have your pick, without competition from me. I'll just sit back and wait for Captain Noah to cruise by."

"I thought you weren't up for taking a chance with any of these guys, Jessica," Penny teased.

Jessica blushed. "Well, to tell you the truth, at first I thought J.L.'s father was right about the locals being strictly a rough crowd. But now that I get a good look at some of these guys..." J.L. and Penny followed Jessica's excited gaze around the room.

"You're right, Jess." J.L. laughed, her voice taking on a more friendly tone. "My dad made it sound like this island turns into a pirates' den at night. But a lot of these guys and girls look exactly like the kids in Connecticut."

"Join us for a drink?" a voice called from a nearby table. All three girls wheeled around clumsily, searching the faces for the source of the voice. Finally J.L. spotted a boy who looked a few years older sitting with two friends at a large table. She nudged Penny and Jessica urgently.

"I don't know," Penny hesitated.

J.L. turned to her. "Nervous, Penny? I think we should join them. Maybe they know Noah."

They look all right to me, Jessica thought to herself. In fact, all three of them are pretty cute. She gave her friends a quick glance to make sure they were following, and took off in the direction of their table.

"Hi," she called, sitting down next to the dark-eyed young man who had invited them over.

"Well, hello," he said, a smile almost as bright as Noah's lighting up his face. "My name's Pete, this is Mark, and this one here's Matt." Jessica nodded to Pete's two sandy-haired companions, who looked like they might be brothers. J.L. and Penny quickly joined the group.

"Are you girls new around here?" Pete continued, gazing at the three girls steadily.

"Well, actually—" Jessica began.

"Yes, we're visiting for a few days," J.L. said, hurrying to be a part of the conversation.

"Visiting, huh? Where from?" asked Mark, the older of the two companions.

"New York," Penny jumped in, before her friends could say "Connecticut." New York just sounds better, she thought.

Pete's eyes flashed. "New York! Well, what brings you here?" He gestured comically around him. "Over the Rainbow isn't exactly a hot spot for tourists."

"Oh, we were invited," Penny answered nonchalantly. "This guy we've been hanging around with since we got here, he invited us. The only trouble is, we can't seem to find him."

"What's his name? Maybe we know him," Matt answered.

"Noah," the girls answered in unison. Matt, Pete, and Mark exchanged a mysterious, snickering look.

"Just Noah?" Pete asked teasingly.

The girls blushed. "Yeah, Noah, the one who has the boat *Aquarius,*" Penny said, trying to hide their obvious enthusiasm.

The boys smiled. "Well, actually we do know him," Mark said. The three girls struggled to keep from showing their eagerness. "In fact, I just saw him." Suddenly his expression changed. "Wait a second, though. If I tell you where he is, you're going to just take off on us, aren't you?"

Jessica stirred uncomfortably, not sure if they were being serious or making fun of them.

"He's in the back, playing pool. I wouldn't interrupt him right now, though," Pete said. "He's a serious pool player, and I hear there's some money riding on the game. What are you drinking?"

The three girls froze.

"Don't worry, it's on us," Pete said, misreading their nervousness. He turned to Penny. "So, what'll it be?"

"Uh, I don't care, whatever you're having, Pete," Penny stammered.

"Same here," Jessica chimed in.

"Sure, why not?" J.L. added.

An understanding look passed among the three young men. "Don't do much drinking back home in New York, do you?" Matt teased. "How about a beer?" The girls nodded in agreement.

"Careful, now," Mark said, leaning toward them. "Beer is very powerful stuff."

"Oh, I'm sure they can handle it," Matt laughed,

speaking in an exaggerated way to his brother. "I mean, I hear up there in New York they do some wicked drugs. I bet these girls do all kinds of drugs, not alcohol — right, girls?"

The three girls laughed a little too quickly.

Matt stood up to get the drinks. He was about to turn toward the bar when a blond girl walked over to the group. She looked about the same age as Jessica, Penny, and J.L. She draped her arms around Matt possessively and looked past him at the girls.

"Hi, Pam," Matt muttered.

"I'm going out for a minute with Janine, but we'll be right back," she said, more for the benefit of the three girls than for Matt. "When we get back we should all get going to that other party." Matt, who did not seem the least bit concerned with this interruption, continued on his way to the bar. The girl lingered for a moment, glaring into Penny's eyes.

Jessica cleared her throat. "So, Pete, do you live in Duck Key?"

"Well, my parents have a cottage here," Pete began. "I live in northern Florida. We all go to the University of Florida in Gainesville. I used to spend the summer here, so I brought my friends down for the long week-end."

"I thought you looked more like college guys than fishermen," J.L. said, relaxing again.

Pete and Mark exchanged another look and laughed. "I'm not sure that's a compliment, J.L.," said Pete.

"How about you?" Mark pressed, glancing at his friend. "Where do you go to school?"

"Collingwood Community College," the three girls answered in a rush. Mark rolled his eyes.

"Colliewood Community College? Is that in New York?"

Just then Matt returned to the table carrying three mugs of beer in each hand. In the commotion, Jessica knocked J.L.'s knee under the table and raised her eyebrow questioningly.

J.L. leaned over and whispered into Jessica's ear. "I know, Jess, I know. I can't figure these guys out either. One second they seem friendly, like they're really interested in us, and the next second I think they're making fun of us. I just wish we could—" J.L. started to say. But she was interrupted when Penny stood up abruptly.

"I'll be right back," Penny announced. She turned her back to the table and looked around the bar.

"Where are you going?" J.L. asked, rising quickly.

"I'm all right," Penny proclaimed confidently. "Don't worry about me." With that, she marched confidently toward the crowd near the bar.

"What's up with your friend?" Matt asked suspiciously.

"I think she just excused herself for a second. She'll be back," Jessica assured him.

Mark turned to watch Penny making her way between the tables. "Hey, the little girls' room is the

other way," he shouted after her. Heads turned, and
J.L. and Jessica couldn't miss the way he emphasized
little girls'. He started to ask them if they liked the
Florida Keys, but Jessica and J.L. were nervously looking around.

By the time Penny reached the bar and glanced back
toward the table, it looked like J.L. and Jessica had
been drawn back into the conversation. Now's my
chance, she thought, suddenly changing course and
starting in the direction of the pool room. Checking
on her friends one last time she stepped through the
doorway, stumbled on an unseen step, and felt someone
catch her.

"Hello, Penny." Noah smiled.

Dammit, why do I have to be so clumsy, Penny
thought to herself. Noah's arms remained around her
shoulders, steadying her.

"If it isn't Captain Noah!" she exclaimed loudly—
too loudly, she realized. "I was just . . . I just thought
I'd take a look around."

Noah looked toward the doorway and asked, "Where
are your friends, L.J. and Jennifer?" Penny smiled to
herself at his mistake. This was working out better
than she had planned.

"Oh, you mean, J.L. and Jessica. They're all tied
up with a couple of college guys. In fact, I think they
forgot all about you."

Noah smiled. "Well, at least one of you remembers
me. I'm really sorry I got hung up on the pool table

for so long. College guys, eh?" he added good-naturedly, starting toward the door.

"Where are we going?" Penny blurted out before she could catch herself.

Noah kept smiling at Penny, unperturbed. "We're going to the bar. I need a refill," he declared with a laugh.

Before Penny could object, Noah was out in the main room, skillfully dodging the groups of people. She finally caught up to him, but when he started to talk to her, the music picked up again. She couldn't hear a word he said. At the bar Noah ordered four beers and a bag of peanuts. Penny glanced over her shoulder to make sure her friends were still wrapped up in their conversation. Then she pushed her way up next to him at the bar.

"Four beers!" she exclaimed, laughing casually. "Noah, you're pretty serious, aren't you? I mean, I heard that sailors drink a lot, but . . ."

Noah turned to her, and their blue eyes met. He grinned at Penny. "First of all, Penny, I'm a fisherman, not a sailor. And second of all, one of these beers is for you," he said, handing Penny a mug. She blushed excitedly. "The extra two," he continued, "are for your friends. Maybe this will at least help them remember me." He laughed, looking over Penny's head in the direction of the table.

"But, Noah, we can't just barge in on them like that," Penny stammered desperately.

"Nonsense," he declared. He swept the three mugs off the bar and started toward the others. Penny hurried to keep up with him. Her face took on the same look of determination it had during important tennis matches. And like any serious tennis player, she wasn't about to give up the advantage she now held over her rivals.

They approached the table. Mark looked up and spotted them first, winking at Penny. He rose and gave Noah a broad, friendly grin. "Look who's here!" he called. J.L. and Jessica turned around, and their mouths dropped in disbelief. Then their expressions changed to anger.

"Yeah, look who's here," J.L. echoed icily.

Penny casually reached an arm around Noah's shoulder. "See what I found," she said, gloating. She first met Jessica's fierce green eyes, then J.L.'s dark eyes, smoking with jealousy. J.L. and Jessica looked from Penny to Noah, who in his white shorts and light blue shirt looked even more tan and gorgeous than they remembered. He reached over them and shook Mark's hand happily.

"Hey, Mark, home on break already?" he asked. Mark laughed, and Noah explained to the others at the table, "When I was in school, it seemed like we never had time off. Seems like you're always on vacation!"

"Just for the weekend," Mark managed to explain through the laughter.

Noah looked around the table, nodding to the others. "Matt, Pete."

Pete nodded. "Hi, Noah. We've been taking care of J.L. and Jessica for you."

"So I see," Noah said, a huge smile lighting his eyes. "Hello there, J.L., Jessica. Sorry I'm late. Is it all right if we join you?"

"Sure, you can join us, Noah," J.L. answered pointedly. She quickly stood and took a seat on the other side of Jessica, leaving one empty seat on each side of the table. Penny, already angry that Pete had provided Noah with her friends' names, flushed visibly. J.L. waited anxiously for Noah to sit in the open chair next to her, but he casually offered it to Penny and sat down between Jessica and Mark. He seemed oblivious of the angry glances going back and forth among the three girls.

"Oh-oh, here comes trouble," he said. The girls who had spoken to Matt earlier had returned with a friend, and Matt and Pete rose to greet them. "Hi, Pam, Janine," Noah said, tossing them a familiar smile.

"I guess we have to get going," Pete explained. "We have another party to go to tonight." Looking right at J.L., Jessica, and Penny, he said, "We'd ask you to join us, but this is going to be a late one—too late for your groupies, I'm afraid."

After what seemed to be an eternity of silence, Noah turned to the girls. "So, I'm really glad you all came.

It's great to see you again. Have any trouble finding the place?"

"Well—" Jessica began.

J.L. interrupted and babbled nervously. "None at all, Noah. How about you?"

Noah laughed heartily. "Oh, I made it all right. I'm starting to know my way around Duck Key, I guess. It's too bad those guys had to leave so quickly, though," he added. "They're friends of mine. They're really nice guys. Pete was just teasing."

"Just teasing, Noah," Jessica jumped in, not about to be cut off again. "He was trying to humiliate us. They said they knew you, but—"

"Well, we went to school together for a while," Noah said, looking at Jessica. He changed the subject and asked instead, "How was Key West? It looks like you got some sun today."

"Fantastic," J.L. proclaimed. "Everything you said it would be. We met Tom, too, and went snorkeling. He talked a lot about you," she added, trying to steer the conversation back to the mysterious Noah.

"How about that sunset?" he asked.

"That was amazing," Penny agreed, finally managing to speak. "The only thing I didn't really like about Key West was the guys."

"You mean the gays?" Noah asked curiously. "Yeah, I know what you mean, Penny. But to each his own, I guess."

J.L., still anxious to find out more about Noah,

broke in, "You went to school with those guys?"

Noah looked confused.

"I mean Matt, Mark, and Pete!" J.L. said, choking with embarrassment.

"Oh, them. I actually met them at the university."

Penny, J.L., and Jessica exchanged a curious look. "You went to college?" Jessica asked, amazed. According to her calculations, that would make him a lot older than they thought he was. Noah cocked his head down and to the side. When he looked up, the familiar smile lit up his features.

"Okay, okay, you all win," he chuckled.

"What do you mean?" asked Jessica defensively.

"Well, I guess it's a part of my nature—you know, my *Aquarian* nature," he added with an even brighter smile. "But I don't really feel comfortable talking about myself. Actually, I think it's pretty boring. I'd much rather find out more about you all." The girls returned Noah's handsome smile.

"We're a lot more boring than you are, Noah," Jessica muttered, looking at him dreamily.

"Speak for yourself, Jessica," said J.L. haughtily, but quickly turned her attention back to the captain.

Noah began, "I *started* college, but I didn't last too long."

"How long?" Penny interrupted. Her two friends shot her a look. Let him talk, their sharp eyes seemed to say.

"Just over a year. I don't know, for some reason

college and I didn't really get along." He suddenly laughed. "I tried to explain that to my parents, but they didn't believe me. They said I got along with everybody else, why couldn't I get along with college?" The three girls laughed appreciatively.

"What were you studying?" J.L. asked.

"Not much, I guess," Noah laughed again. "Or really, I *was* studying, but not the things they wanted me to study. I guess from the first time my uncle took me out in his skiff, I knew what I wanted to do. I took a few business courses, but pretty soon I decided college couldn't teach me much more about what I wanted to know. So I quit." He paused for a long moment. The three girls gazed at him admiringly.

"Not that college is a bad thing. I missed it as soon as I dropped out. It's great to be away from home with all those people your own age. 'Course I don't have to tell you about that," he added with a sly smile. "But then my uncle died and left me the boat."

"Noah. Hey Noah!" The captain looked up suddenly as someone called from across the room.

"That's right," he said apologetically, "I left another quarter on the pool table. It must be my game." He gave the three girls a warm look. "I promise I'll lose quickly and be right back," he said, starting away.

All at once he stopped, and turned back to the table. "I just remembered that Matt was supposed to play this one with me, but he left. Who wants to be my partner?"

"I'd love to," Jessica shrieked, practically knocking over her chair as she raced after Noah. J.L. and Penny watched as Jessica and the tanned hunk headed toward the pool room.

11

Noah quickly discovered that Jessica wasn't a natural at pool. She stood next to him and watched as their opponents, a pair of tough, unfriendly-looking young men, rammed ball after ball into the pockets. Pete was right, Jessica thought. They take their pool very seriously around here—like Show No Mercy. They were being beaten badly and quickly. She glanced at Noah, who winked at her nonchalantly. He didn't seem to care, and Jessica was too caught up with the captain of the *Aquarius* to be embarrassed.

One of their opponents finally missed a shot and handed the cue stick to Jessica. "Your shot, girl," he said gruffly. Jessica ignored him and took the battered stick. She walked to the table in her most sophisticated manner and waited for Noah.

"Okay, Jess," said the tanned Aquarian. He flashed his wide, bright smile. Noah looked over the arrangement of the balls left on the table. As Jessica watched him, she felt like forgetting the game completely. She just wanted to throw her arms around his dark neck, but tried desperately to hide her excitement. He seemed to make up his mind, and announced, "It looks like the six should be straight in."

Jessica looked up at him uncomprehendingly.

Noah smiled again and moved closer to her. "It's easy," he laughed. "Just put the six ball into that corner pocket. Here, I'll help you line it up."

"No, I can do it," Jessica pretended to insist. She leaned over and clumsily acted like she was lining up the shot Noah had picked out for her. After a second she stood up and smiled coyly. "Okay, I guess I could use a hand."

She leaned over again and Noah hunched over her, putting one hand gently on each one of Jessica's hands on the cue stick. Jessica couldn't help letting out a little gasp when she realized she was almost surrounded by the man of her dreams. Good things come in small packages, she repeated to herself, then added hopefully: I really think he likes me. When he took his hands off hers, she pushed the cue stick forward as if in a dream. Jessica couldn't believe it when the six ball rolled into the corner pocket.

"Hey, hey!" Noah exclaimed, putting an arm over her shoulder and giving her a little hug. "That's it! And you get to shoot again!"

Jessica looked into his face, flashing her big green eyes. "Do I have to?"

Penny and J.L. walked into the room. They watched jealously as the gorgeous skipper leaned over and lined up another shot for Jessica. J.L.'s anger at Penny faded.

Both were comrades in jealousy now. Jessica's second shot missed by a mile, but she didn't seem to care. She giggled wildly. One of the tough-looking guys snatched the cue stick from her and quickly finished the game.

"Disgusting!" Penny sputtered.

"Hey, J.L., Penny, I didn't see you two come in," Noah said. "Did you catch the game? Jessica was great, wasn't she?"

Penny glared at the beaming redhead and said, "Yeah, a regular Minnesota *Fats!*" Her voice sounded like breaking glass.

"I thought you lost," J.L. finally added flatly.

Jessica regarded her irate friends with satisfaction. I don't know, I consider it quite a victory, she gloated to herself. Look what I won. She casually slung an arm up over Noah's shoulder. "I think we'll make a pretty good team," she announced.

J.L. choked on her beer.

"Listen, stay right here. I'm just going to make a quick phone call," Noah announced, starting for the back door of the bar.

J.L. saw her chance. Still coughing, she jumped to her feet and brushed past Jessica. "Noah, wait!" she called. "I could use some fresh air."

Jessica and Penny watched helplessly as the tall brunette raced after the blond hunk. Noah paused in the doorway, holding the door for her.

They stepped out into the parking lot and started toward a pay phone on the corner.

As J.L. walked alongside Noah, she took a deep breath of the ocean air. "Ah," she purred, "finally a chance to talk."

Noah gave a sympathetic chuckle. "Yeah, it's not so easy in that place, is it—with the music and that crowd!"

"There are a few distractions," J.L. agreed in a friendly voice.

Noah didn't seem to detect her meaning. As they walked, J.L. studied his handsome face. When she finally looked ahead, she saw that they had nearly reached the phone booth.

"So, Noah—" she began again. But she cut herself off when she realized that she didn't know what she was going to say. She stopped walking and turned to him. A soft light that hung above the phone booth shone on his face, highlighting his features. His deep blue eyes glistened, reminding J.L. of the sea, which she heard beating on the shore nearby. Under his captivating gaze she felt her confidence and Scorpio determination building. J.L. began again, her voice automatically dropping a notch in breathless excitement. "I can't believe I have to leave tomorrow."

"I can't either," said Noah. J.L. searched his face for signs of disappointment. She was sure she had detected a note of sadness in his voice.

"I mean . . ." she started, taking a slight step toward him.

Noah seemed to smile encouragingly. "You know, something in my horoscope today made me think of you," he said. J.L. waited tensely, her whole body alive. "It said, 'A friend who leaves tomorrow won't go as far away as you thought.'" J.L. stood facing the captain, wondering what he meant. She waited for him to continue. But when Noah didn't say anything else, she reached out and took his hand. He laughed and squeezed it affectionately. "I don't know, it's just been really great meeting you—all of you. I really love my job, but I have to admit I get tired of the usual tourists I take out on the Aquarius. And I know you'd get along really well with Melissa. Oh, that reminds me . . ." He laughed, withdrawing his hand and digging in the pocket of his shorts. "I forgot what I was supposed to be doing. Hang on a second, J.L. I'll call her and see if she can make it over here."

J.L. watched incredulously as Noah produced some change and abruptly turned toward the phone booth. He dropped the coins in the slot and started dialing a number.

"Melissa?" J.L. stammered.

"Yeah, she's my girlfriend." Noah began smiling excitedly. Noticing the confused expression on J.L.'s face, he quickly added, "I told you about her, didn't I? I didn't? Well, she works in a restaurant and gets off at twelve. I'll try to convince her to come over, J.L. She usually hates my friends, but I know she'll like you all a lot."

J.L. tried to speak, but stood there stupidly. She felt her shock turn suddenly to embarrassment. "I'd better go back," she said as she started toward the bar.

"I'll be right in, J.L.," Noah called after her casually.

She took a deep breath and walked back through the doorway of the bar. She found Penny and Jessica in the main room. Penny shot her a hostile look, but because of the loud rock and roll, J.L. couldn't hear what she said. She stood silently for a few minutes, trying to recover her composure and readjust to the chaos.

Jessica noticed the strange expression on J.L.'s face. "What's wrong, J.L.?" she finally asked.

"He has a girlfriend!" J.L. blurted out, plenty loud enough to be heard above the music. Penny and Jessica froze. A few heads nearby wheeled around curiously.

"What?" Jessica mouthed.

"Yeah, some Melissa something-or-other," J.L. hissed derisively, venting her frustration.

Penny grew defiant. "How do you know?" she demanded.

"Who do you think he's calling? He wants her to come over here after work and meet us."

"Why, that . . ." Penny sputtered.

J.L. sighed. "He says he thought he told us about her. He says we'd get along just great."

Jessica looked sick. "Let's get out of here," she said urgently.

Penny stiffened. "What? Jessica, we can't leave now. We'd look like fools, like we were running away."

"You're right, Penny," J.L. agreed, that familiar, determined look settling across her features. "I say we stay and show Noah what he's missing."

"He'll be sorry he's stuck with this Melissa before I leave here tonight," Penny promised. Jessica looked helplessly from the dark Scorpio to the blond Sagittarian. She knew them well and knew they both had dangerous tempers. Penny was looking around the bar aggressively. Jessica watched nervously as the tall tennis player caught the eyes of two young men who were leaning against the bar. They smiled, picked up fresh drinks, and started toward the girls.

"Oh-oh," Jessica muttered as soon as she could see what was happening. "J.L.," she called. "I don't know if this is such a good idea," she warned weakly.

"Jessica Holly, we'll show Captain Noah he's not the only handsome guy in the Keys," J.L. proclaimed, watching the two approaching men. "These guys are cute!"

"Uh, J.L., I have the feeling they're not your type," Jessica pursued.

"No, hang on, Jessica. I just want Noah to see this. Maybe then he'll realize what he's missing in J.L. Richter!"

The two men had pushed their way through the crowd. They bumped hard into J.L. and Jessica, and crashed into the middle of the girls' conversation.

"Well, hello," one of them drawled, nodding at J.L. and Jessica, and smiling broadly at Penny. "My name's Ron. This is my friend Al."

Great, Jessica thought to herself as she watched

Penny and J.L. introduce themselves to the newcomers. Ron was a tall, broad-shouldered young man, maybe twenty-five, Jessica guessed. He was handsome, all right, but he was dressed in tight jeans and T-shirt and one of the sleeves was rolled around a pack of cigarettes, like the tough guys in the movies. She almost laughed out loud, except there was something about him that seemed threatening. His eyes seemed too quick and hard to follow when he looked from Penny to J.L., in spite of the friendly conversation. Ron's friend Al looked even tougher, but Jessica assured herself it was mostly the tinted glasses and army-style crew cut that did it. Unlike Ron and most of the other guys in the bar, Al looked pale as a ghost, as if he hadn't stepped outside in months. "Yeah, great choice, Penny," she moaned, and braced herself.

". . . ahem, and this is Jessica," Penny shouted, repeating the introduction she had just missed. Jessica looked back to Ron, who was holding out his hand and looking her over. This time, though, Jessica knew exactly what he was looking at. She quickly recovered and shot out her hand.

"That's right, Jessica. Looking for something?" she added, following his eyes down her body. "Well?" she challenged him again. Their eyes met, and a slight blush tinged the young man's ears. He abruptly turned back to Penny. "And hiya, Al," Jessica continued, playfully slapping the other young man on the shoulder. "What's the matter, Al, cat got your tongue?"

Al stared at Jessica for a second, then turned to J.L. "Your friend has quite a sense of humor," he remarked dully. J.L. shot Jessica a look that practically screamed "Shut up!"

Jessica shrugged and buried her snicker inside her glass of beer.

"So, what d'ya say?" Al said to Penny, moving closer to her side and giving her another once-over.

"I don't know. What do *you* say?" Penny replied with a smile, but instinctively took a step backward. She bumped into a girl's elbow, causing both Penny and the girl to spill their drinks. Penny quickly turned to her to apologize but was met by a disdainful face. Ron stepped in, pulling Penny toward him. Penny and J.L. exchanged a quick, nervous look.

"So," Ron tried to continue his conversation with Penny nonchalantly, "having a good time?"

"Not bad," Penny managed to say, glancing at her companions. But the excited note had disappeared from her voice. "Umm . . . how about you?" she added as an afterthought.

"Just dandy, Penny." He took another step toward her, and addressed both Penny and J.L. "How about getting rid of little sis, so we can really have a party?" he urged, tilting his head to indicate Jessica.

"What!" Penny exclaimed, pulling her arm out of his grasp.

"You heard me," he continued, loud enough for Jessica to hear. "Why don't you send her home to Mommy and Daddy, so it'll be just you, me, Al, and J.L. We could go for a ride . . ." As the music stopped and his words hit her, Penny glanced over at Jessica, who was gaping at the two men. She shook her head in amazement.

"I don't think so!" J.L. stammered, first to Al, then to Ron.

"What's the matter, girls?" Ron continued innocently.

"I think this conversation is over," Penny announced.

He smiled rudely. "Did you hear that, Al? She thinks the conversation is over."

In spite of the tension of the moment, Jessica could barely stifle a laugh. "I didn't realize the conversation had even started for Al," she giggled. The music began again. Al and Ron exchanged a look.

"Yeah, pretty funny for a chick with a torn sweatshirt and pants that are too short," Ron snorted.

"Hey, knock it off—" Penny began, but Ron wheeled to face her.

"What?" he asked menacingly. "What do you mean, knock it off? Wasn't it you who invited us over here in the first place? What did you expect? Just a little friendly chitchat?" Penny ducked between them and stepped toward her friends.

"Aw, look at 'em, Al," Ron chided the three girls.

"The three women in the tub. The preppy, the beggar, and the—"

"Don't you dare say it!" J.L. screamed angrily as Ron pointed to her miniskirt.

Suddenly Jessica sighed heavily, her knees buckled, and she crumpled to the floor.

"Jessica!" J.L. and Penny exclaimed together.

Ron and Al looked at Jessica on the floor, then at J.L. and Penny. Their expressions turned to fear.

J.L. and Penny knelt beside Jessica. J.L. leaned over Jessica's face and whispered, "Jessica? If you can hear me, exhale." J.L. felt Jessica's breath across her neck. This is an act, right?" she muttered cautiously under her breath. "I thought you'd retired the fainting bit for good!" She looked over at Penny, careful not to let Ron and Al see the wink she gave her. Together Penny and J.L. pretended to aid their friend, gently lifting her head in their arms.

"Is she all right?" Ron finally managed to ask. Penny looked up at the two men's confused faces. A small circle had cleared around the girls, and people craned to see the apparently unconscious redhead. A young woman pushed between the two men. She leaned over the girls.

"I'll get the bartender," she offered.

"No!" J.L. began, then caught herself. It was all Jessica could do to keep a straight face as she heard J.L. continue, "I mean, it wouldn't do any good. Jessica got too much sun today—you should see how burned she is," she confided to the concerned young woman. "I think it's probably sunstroke or something. She's so fair. We should probably just get her some air, get her out this hot place."

Jessica rolled her head from side to side and moaned. Slowly she opened her eyes and looked around her, as if trying to regain full consciousness. She blinked several times at Penny, then sighed heavily.

The young woman pressed J.L. "You should really let me get the bartender. He'll know if—"

J.L. rose and faced her, leaving Penny with Jessica, who seemed to be recovering slowly but surely. "Thank you very much." J.L. smiled at the woman. "But I really think the best thing is just for us to get her out of here and into the fresh air. It's awful in here," she said, casting an angry glance at Ron and Al.

"Uh, is she all right?" Ron asked again.

"Yes, she'll be fine, I think," J.L. coldly assured them, then turned back to Jessica and Penny. Jessica was sitting up now, and the small crowd began to turn away. As soon as they were convinced Jessica was probably going to be fine, Al and Ron quickly retreated into the crowd. The young woman remained for a moment, eyeing the girls, but soon she, too, turned back to her group of friends. The girls were left to themselves.

Jessica continued her act even though nobody was watching. "I . . . I . . . I don't remember a thing," she mumbled, shaking her head. "I must have fainted.

Oh, dear, it must have caused such a scene!"

Penny and J.L. tried to restrain their laughter.

"Well, actually, Jessica, you had a pretty small audience this time," J.L. confided as they helped her to her feet. "It's so crowded in here that only the people jammed in close to us really saw anything. But come on, now, we're supposed to be getting you out of here!"

They fought their way through the bar. At last they neared the door and could smell the cool evening air mixing with the thick smoke of the stuffy bar. Jessica inhaled deeply and laughed. She nearly forgot that she was supposed to still be recovering. J.L. saw that Jessica was beginning to act a little too lively and gave her a light smack right on her sunburn.

"Ouch! J.L., what did you do that for?" she protested. Before J.L. could say anything, Noah's voice broke in.

"Hey, you aren't leaving?" All three girls looked up at once. Gorgeous as ever, Noah waited by the door— but there was no trace of his usual smile. Jessica completely forgot about the fainting act and J.L. and Penny shuffled nervously. "Were you just going to leave without saying anything? Melissa's on her way . . ." he objected. When he mentioned his girlfriend's name, Penny felt her anger rising.

"Tell her we're very sorry we couldn't stay," said Penny sarcastically.

"What Penny means," J.L. jumped in, "is that we have to leave tomorrow, and it has been a long day, and Jess doesn't feel well—right, Jess?" Jessica nodded. "And you're right. We should have looked for you. It was really thoughtless of us."

"Well," he said sadly, "it's really too bad you're leaving already." His keen gaze lingered for a moment on each of the girls' faces. There was an uncomfortable pause. Penny, J.L., and Jessica felt a sudden unexpected wave of regret replacing their jealousy and anger. "Good-bye, I've enjoyed meeting you, and I hope you come back again."

He turned to leave, and then stopped. Pointing to Jessica, he said, "Virgo, right?" Jessica's face broke into a delighted smile and she nodded. "And Penny, the athlete, you're a Sagittarius. Am I correct?"

"Yes!" Penny confirmed, amazed.

"And you, J.L.? I'm afraid I never did quite figure you out."

"I'm a Scorpio," J.L. said quietly, and smiled.

"Well, what do you know?" he said. He turned, still shaking his head, and disappeared into the bar.

Jessica stared at the open door. "He's so gorgeous," she mumbled.

"See, he really did like us," Penny said. "Not quite in the way we hoped, but as friends. And that's more than we were being to each other."

"What do you mean?" J.L. asked.

"We were all so busy trying to get Noah's attention, we acted like jerks—in front of all those people and to each other."

"I guess you're right," Jessica agreed. "The Zodiacs would not have been pleased with us. We would have gotten an Abby Martin lecture on 'friendship.' Still, Noah is a great guy and it's a compliment to us that he liked us, even if it was just as friends."

"Come on," J.L. urged. "We'd better get back." The three girls linked arms and started off toward the cottage.

They walked down the dark streets in silence.

At last J.L. spoke. "Well, so much for our beautiful Aquarian."

"That's what we should have said hours ago," Jessica said softly. "Some of us know when to give up," she added, glaring at Penny. Penny looked guiltily from J.L. to Jessica, and the three fell silent again.

"Well, Jessica, the fainting bit helped," J.L. began a few moments later, "but Penny and I could have handled ourselves with Ron and Al."

"Sure," Jessica murmured.

The three continued walking. They reached the cottage, but deliberately kept walking and continued onto the beach. The nearly full moon had broken out of the clouds, and they could easily see up and down the long stretch of sand.

"J.L., maybe if you hadn't dressed so . . ." Penny began, but broke off as soon as she realized what she was saying.

Jessica burst into a fit of laughter, and soon J.L. and Penny were also holding their sides and sitting in the sand. After an hour and a half of the tense bar scene, it felt so good just to giggle hysterically now. "You guys," Jessica said, gasping for air and slowly turning serious. "You know we're just lucky to have gotten out of there when we did."

"I know!" J.L. agreed. "You were right all along. We really didn't belong in that situation. But I guess I was too proud to admit it."

"Sure, J.L.," Penny objected, "but I was the one who insisted on staying. I guess I owe you an apology—"

"No way!" Jessica declared. "We all got ourselves into it, and we all got out of it okay—and together. Maybe not with the greatest of ease," she added, smiling, "but we got out of it. I'm only sorry about one thing."

"Oh-oh," J.L. laughed, sensing one of Jessica's jokes. "What's that?"

"I'm sorry that Noah missed his only chance to fall in love with me. I hate to think of him stuck in a miserable life with this Melissa character."

J.L. turned to Penny. "Delusions. Occasionally follow the fainting spell, but usually clear up by the next morning." The girls laughed. They sat on the beach listening to the soothing sound of the breakers on the beach. It was high tide again, and the waves moved far up on the beach, nearly reaching the girls. They broke loudly over the sand, but the sound was so peaceful after the din of the party. Finally J.L. decided it was time to head back to the house.

"What time are we getting up tomorrow?" Penny asked as she stood and stretched.

"Who knows? Dad said we'll have to leave here about noon," J.L. groaned.

The three girls walked slowly back to the cottage, wading in the cool ocean water. As they turned and climbed toward the house, J.L. hurried ahead to hold on to the slamming door.

"I'll take care of this," she whispered as Jessica and Penny filed past her. "We've had plenty of adventures for one night."

12

It seemed as if the girls had just closed their eyes when they became aware of Mrs. Richter opening the shades and calling, "Come on, girls, we have a plane to catch."

She surveyed the room, taking in the scattered party clothes and makeup. "Hmm, it looks like I missed a little excitement last night."

J.L. sat up suddenly. "Uh, we just had to make sure we had all our stuff, Mom," she offered, weakly rubbing the sleep out of her eyes.

Mrs. Richter paused at the door and said over her shoulder, "Well, if your inventory has been completed, you girls better get packed. Dad wants to leave in an hour." J.L. stared after her nervously. She couldn't tell from her mother's reaction whether she intended to tell J.L.'s father that she suspected that they had been out the night before or to let it pass.

"Looks like we weren't as clever as we thought," said J.L. glumly. "I can't believe we forgot to clean up when we got home last night."

Jessica yawned. "I was so tired by the time we got back here I don't think I could have cleaned up one piece of clothing. Anyhow, it looks just like my room at home."

Penny sat up, shook her long blond hair, and reached for her hairbrush. "I wonder what Melissa's like?" she said, unable to take her mind away from Noah. Then she tossed her head proudly, declaring, "Well, whoever she is, I'll bet she doesn't have anything on us."

Jessica laughed. "Personally, I don't want to think about her . . . but I sure would like to know more about what was going on inside that Aquarius head of his. Hey, maybe we'll get a clue from this!" She pulled the astrological guide from her suitcase.

This time, instead of skimming the paragraphs, she read them slowly. J.L. and Penny watched her impatiently.

"C'mon, Jess," J.L. urged, "are you going to read it or what?"

Jessica cleared her throat dramatically and began. "*'The Aquarian Man: His interests are scattered all over the place. That's because his love of people is so impersonal; he gives a certain value to everyone he meets, while the rest of us save such efforts for only the very special people in our lives. To an Aquarian, everyone is special, and I mean everyone. Even those he hasn't met yet. Few Uranus men are ever selfish or petty.'* See?" Jessica said, a small note of triumph in her voice. "He *was* our friend. But it's like Tom said yesterday when we went snorkeling. Noah's everybody's friend, from here to Miami."

"Give me that," Penny said, grabbing the book from

Jessica. Her eyes raced across the pages. Suddenly she let out a long, deep laugh. "It's all right here. *'He'll cling to the illusion that he's involved in a nice, safe platonic friendship, long after a palsy-walsy relationship has become impossible for you.'* How true!"

The three girls sighed in unison.

"Well, we'd better get moving," J.L. said. "My dad does not appreciate being kept waiting."

The girls dressed and packed in no time. J.L. organized the cleanup operation in the bedroom. Jessica changed the sheets, J.L. dusted and arranged the furniture, and Penny vacuumed.

"Hey, look what I just found!" J.L. and Jessica turned to see Penny holding a page from the local newspaper Jessica had bought their first day on the island. "It's our horoscopes for the weekend. Remember these? Let's see how accurate they really were. Who's first?"

"Read your own, Penny," Jessica suggested.

"*'Sagittarius: There may be opposition to your plans this weekend. A party held this evening might be more rewarding than one held over the next four evenings. Confusion in romantic scene may cause entanglements with a true friend.'*" She looked over at her companions and waited for their reaction.

"Not too bad," Jessica mused. "What about mine?"

Penny read, "*'Virgo: You gain from taking a peaceful, amicable, and cooperative attitude. You will meet someone, but may get more from a quiet atmosphere where you can really talk to those you love. Moon in opposition to Mars indicates stressful situations might lead to physical complications.'"*

All three girls laughed hysterically. "Physical complications!" J.L. sputtered. "That's perfect! When you crashed to the floor last night . . ." J.L. doubled over in renewed fits of laughter. Penny wiped the tears from her eyes.

"Jessica, one thing about this is right," Penny said. "You were certainly the peacekeeper this weekend. J.L. and I should have spent more time listening to your suggestions."

Jessica blushed. "Aw, I wasn't so sharp myself sometimes. But what about that business of meeting somebody. It's always like that for me. I'm always meeting somebody, but there's never any romance."

"According to this, you were looking in the wrong places. You shouldn't have expected to find romance in Over the Rainbow." Penny turned to J.L. "J.L., here goes: *'Scorpio: You may promise and commit yourself to an uncomfortable situation. Evening is ideal for romance, courtship, creative activities, seeing people in groups. Possible conflict with authority figures.'"*

J.L. pretended to mop her brow. "Yeah, conflict with authority figures, all right. It's a good thing Mom seems to be keeping quiet about our little adventure last night."

"But I think Penny and I owe you an apology—" Jessica began.

"Oh, no, Jess. I was the one who really insisted that we ignore my father's advice—"

"No, J.L.," Jessica interrupted with an impish smile. "I mean that according to your horoscope we should have let you stay last night. Maybe Silent Al really was the man for you."

J.L. grabbed a pillow and sent it flying in Jessica's direction. But Mr. Richter barged through the door.

"Quit the horseplay, girls," he ordered sternly. One look at his face told J.L. that he knew that they had been out last night. Oh-oh, she thought to herself. She shot her two friends a look which said: "I'll handle this," and braced herself for her father's anger.

"Aren't you ready yet?" he asked, looking around the room.

J.L. stood up. "We just finished cleaning," she stated, and picked up her suitcase. "I guess that's everything."

"Well, before you load your bags in the car . . ." Mr. Richter began. J.L. set the suitcase down and stood facing her father. "I'd like to say a few things to you." Penny cleared her throat, and she and Jessica glanced at each other nervously.

"Where did you go last night, J.L.?" Mr. Richter asked directly.

J.L. sighed, took a deep breath, and prepared to tell her father about their trip to Over the Rainbow. But then Mr. Richter changed his mind. "No, let me start again." He looked hard at each of the girls.

"J.L., Penny, Jessica, we heard a door slam last night, and when I came down here I discovered that you had all left the house." The three girls lowered their eyes to the floor guiltily. He continued, "Now, I didn't want to end this vacation on a sour note, but your little adventure last night cost Mrs. Richter and me a lot of worry and lost sleep. J.L., I thought we had an understanding."

"We did," J.L. asserted.

"Well, I don't know how this thing last night fits into that agreement." J.L. looked up and met his eyes. They stared at each other a moment. She thought she saw his angry expression relax slightly. "Unless, of course, you all just went for a last walk on the beach."

J.L. glanced quickly at her friends, then back at her father. "That's what we did, Dad," she said calmly, grateful to have the opportunity to use this half-truth. J.L. saw disbelief on her father's face, but also saw that he was allowing her this opportunity. "Besides," she blurted out, "you told us to use our own good judgment. I can assure you we really did, Dad."

Mr. Richter looked from J.L. to Penny and Jessica, then back to his daughter. "Well, I think I've said all that I will say. We understand each other, right, girls? Now, finish up in here. We're leaving in three minutes." He turned quickly and left the room.

"We'd better hurry," J.L. said quietly. The three girls exchanged knowing looks, gathered their bags, and hurried out to the car.

"Anne, you drive for a while. I'm a bit tired," Mr. Richter said, turning with a slight smile to the three girls in the back seat.

The three exchanged looks of relief and settled in for the drive to the airport. As they passed the marina, they looked to see if they could find the *Aquarius* one last time.

"Looking for someone special?" J.L. asked Jessica.

"No, just taking a last look," Jessica answered.

"We all wish we could see the *Aquarius,* if you know what I mean!" Penny added.

"We should get the story straight before the next Zodiac meeting!" said J.L., and they all laughed.

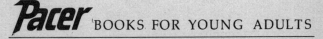

Join THE ZODIAC CLUB

_You can be part of THE ZODIAC CLUB.
Share the fun and adventures
with the founding members._

Just fill out and return the coupon below
and you will receive:

★ **membership card** ★
★ **free personalized computerized horoscope** ★
★ **upcoming news of Zodiac Club titles** ★
★ **and more surprises** ★

_____ Yes! Enroll me in THE ZODIAC CLUB

Please send me my free personalized
computerized horoscope.

Name _____ Age _____
Address _____
City/State _____ Zip _____
Birthdate _____
　　　　　Day　　　　　Month　　　　　Year
　　　　　　　　　A.M.
Time of birth _____ P.M. Place of birth _____
　　　　　　　　　　　　　　　　　City　　State

Please enclose $1.50 to cover postage and handling.
Send check or money order — no cash or C.O.D.'s
please.

MAIL TO:　Box Zodiac 7
　　　　　Pacer Books
　　　　　The Putnam Publishing Group
　　　　　51 Madison Avenue New York, NY 10010